Salvation

ANGEL'S HALO
Next Gen

USA Today Bestselling Author

TERRI ANNE
BROWNING

Salvation
Written by Terri Anne Browning
All Rights Reserved ©Terri Anne Browning 2019
Cover Design and Photo by Sara Eirew
Edited by Lisa Hollett of Silently Correcting Your Grammar
Formatting by M.L. Pahl of IndieVention Designs

ISBN: 9781080562435

10 9 8 7 6 5 4 3 2 1

Salvation

ONE

Fighting back a yawn, I walked into the kitchen, my nose following the smell of coffee. I'd heard low murmurs as I'd made my way through the living room, but as soon as the door opened, they stopped abruptly. I instantly went on high alert without the need for caffeine.

Balling my hands into fists to keep my fingers from shaking, I took in who was in the room. Dad was at the kitchen table, which was weird because he was normally out the door by five thirty during the week. He co-owned the auto and bike shop, and they opened at a ridiculous hour to "accommodate the working man," as he liked to say. From six in the morning to six in the evening, he and his partner took care of the entire county's automotive needs.

Dad had his chair turned to face Mom, who sat at the table with her hands clenched so tightly around her coffee mug, her knuckles were white. That and her bloodless lips were the only things that told me something was definitely off with her.

Across from her, Uncle Jet and Aunt Flick sat with their own chairs pulled close together. The oldest of my mom's brothers had one arm around his wife, the other hand holding his coffee mug he'd half lifted to his mouth but seemed to have forgotten all about midway to its destination.

Even without the abrupt way their conversation cut off, I would have known something was up simply because no one was eating. Aunt Flick normally made breakfast for everyone, and if Mom was home, she would help. But there was no lingering smell of fried bacon permeating the air, not even a single leftover biscuit.

Heart pounding, I cautiously walked toward the table even though every instinct in my body was screaming for me to run. Whatever these four had been talking about wasn't good, and I wasn't sure I wanted to know. But when Mom's green eyes caught mine and I saw the flash of fear—oh fuck, fear in Raven Hannigan's eyes—I knew I couldn't run from what was about to come.

"What's wrong?" I demanded, my eyes never once leaving the woman I loved more than life.

As I watched, she forced herself to relax her hands, but it took several seconds for the blood flow to return to her fingers. Pasting on a smile that didn't even begin to relieve some of my own fear, she shook her blond head. "Nothing is wrong, silly," she lied.

"Mom," I began, but Dad stood, his big frame blocking her from my eyes for a moment as he meticulously pushed in his chair before crossing to the coffeepot and taking down my favorite mug.

When I saw Mom's face again, she was her normal self once more, and that bothered me more than anything else in this warped nightmare I'd just walked into.

Mug full, Dad brought it back to me and kissed the top of my head. "Mom and I are going to be out today. We have a few errands to run that can't wait. I was hoping you could take care of the office today since we're both going to be gone and Trigger has no people skills."

I wanted to yell at him to stop acting and tell me what the hell was going on, but instead, I found myself nodding. Because if I were honest, I was fucking terrified of what they would say if they actually did tell me the truth.

The night before flashed through my mind, making my stomach clench, and I put my coffee on the table without taking a drink. No way was I going to think about the night before. They couldn't possibly have known what I'd been doing, and with whom. And they never would.

"No problem," I assured him as I hugged him with both arms. When I felt him tremble, I almost threw up then and there.

Something is very, very wrong.

All the way to the shop, those five words kept repeating like a mantra in my head. When I pulled into the parking lot, driving around to the back where all the employees kept their vehicles, I noticed the shop was already full of customers.

Thankful for the distraction, I ran inside, putting on my best smile as I did. "Good morning," I said as I hurried through the shop to the counter.

"Sorry I'm late. Mom and Dad didn't let me know they needed me today until the last minute."

"Lexa dear," Mrs. Johnston greeted me with a warm smile, first in line. "Good to see you home. How did college life treat you?"

Making sure my hair stayed over the right side of my face, I returned her smile. "It was great. It was nice to get away for a little while."

"Raven was just telling me a few months ago that you made the dean's list your first semester at Oregon. She's so proud of you, she could burst."

"That's my mom," I said with a laugh. Pulling up the right files for her, I quickly checked her out and handed over the keys to her car. "Good to see you, ma'am."

It took twenty minutes to get everyone waiting out the door. As soon as the shop was clear, I walked out into the garage to check on everyone. When Dad and Trigger took over the shop after Uncle Jack died, they expanded the garage to ten bays and hired more mechanics. Yet they still couldn't seem to keep up with all the business they had.

"Morning, Lexa," Trigger called as he wiped his grease-covered hands on a stained rag.

"Morning," I returned, glancing around at the others hard at work in their own bays. "Do you have any order forms I need to take care of? And if you guys want me to call in lunch orders, make sure to have them ready by ten thirty."

"I think Raven took care of everything last night before she left. She stayed a little later than usual to tie up any loose ends so you wouldn't have to deal with them this week."

"This week?" I repeated, confused. "Dad didn't mention the rest of the week. He just asked me to cover for him and Mom today."

He shrugged. "Bash said Raven would be out all week. Just assumed you would be covering for her during that time."

"I will. I don't mind. They just didn't mention it, is all." Frustrated because my concern for my parents was only escalating, I started straightening up my dad's bay, needing something to do. He usually only worked on classic vehicles and bikes, and he kept his work area pristine, but I felt an urgent need to do something with my hands. "Did they mention why Mom was taking the week off."

"No. But it was something that came up all of a sudden, so who knows with our queen, right?"

Giving me a grim smile, he excused himself and walked back to his own bay.

"Yeah," I muttered to myself as I returned to the shop. "Who knows with her."

The rest of the morning went by without any issues. The pace was steady, and in between customers, I cleaned the shop even though it wasn't the least bit dirty. After calling in everyone's lunch order, I left the shop an hour later to pick it up.

As soon as I walked through the door at Aggie's, memories of the night before assaulted me, and I avoided looking around as I crossed to the counter. It didn't surprise me that my aunt Quinn was already there, even though she'd been working the evening before. Ever since Aggie had made her a partner in the diner and started taking more and more time off, Quinn always seemed to be there.

The perky blonde beamed at me as I approached her. "Well, this is nice. I get to see you two days in a row. What can I do for you, lovely girl?"

"I'm picking up the huge call-in order for the guys at the shop," I told her. "I'm covering for Mom this week."

"Ah, okay. Give me like five minutes, and I'll get everything together. We've been swamped with call-in orders. Apparently, the entire police department called in one too." Even as she was talking, the bell over the entrance went off, and I felt every fine hair on my body lift. "Looks like everyone is arriving all at once to pick up their orders. Afternoon, Sheriff."

I felt Ben more and more the closer he came until my entire body was vibrating with anticipation. His deep voice sounded like it was right beside my ear when he spoke. "Quinn." He stepped in close to the counter, his side brushing against mine. "Lexa," he murmured.

Closing my eyes, I savored the sound of my name coming from him, even as my heart clenched so painfully, it was hard to draw in a deep enough breath for a moment. "Sheriff," I gritted out, sidestepping so he wasn't touching me.

When I opened my eyes, they lingered on him, taking in his short, dark hair, that strong jaw and broad nose. The urge to lick his lips hit me all over again, stronger than it had been the night before. After I forced my eyes away from those lips, they went straight to his wide shoulders encased in his work uniform, then down to his tapered waist with his belt that had his revolver, flashlight, and a radio attached to it. Damn it, he made that uniform look so freaking good, there should have been a law against it.

Thankfully, Quinn didn't seem to notice our interaction, or the fact that I was drooling over the guy who'd so effortlessly shattered me without even a word the night before. "Like I was telling Lexa, Sheriff, we've had a lot of large call-in orders today. Give me a few minutes, and I'll get you taken care of."

"Take your time," he told her, and even though I refused to look at him, I knew his eyes were on me. "I'm in no hurry."

Giving him her signature beaming smile, Quinn went into the kitchen to gather our food.

The restaurant was crowded with hungry customers, but suddenly, I felt alone with Ben right beside me. It was just the two of us in the universe for a single moment, and I craved for the situation to be different so I could have the one thing I knew I never could.

When his fingers skimmed down my arm, I shivered, then quickly jerked back and looked around to make sure no had noticed him touching me. "Don't," I hissed.

"We need to talk." He said it casually and just loud enough for those nearest to hear. "You left before we could discuss everything."

Brushing the hair back from the right side of my face, I turned so he could see what I'd shown him the night before. The scar that had so disgusted him he'd been left speechless and I'd been shattered.

His eyes landed on it and darkened. Last night, I hadn't gotten a good enough look in the dark to see what color his eyes were, but I could see them all too clearly now. They were a brandy brown, and after the kiss we'd shared the night before, I knew he could be just as smooth and intoxicating as his eyes promised.

"Tell me who did that to you," he commanded, stepping closer and lowering his voice so only I could hear.

The savage fury in his voice made me shiver again, but it didn't frighten me. I'd faced scarier men than him in my lifetime.

Stepping back, I tucked my hair back down over the right side of my face, hiding the scar that went from my temple to the corner of my mouth. "That isn't any of your business, Sheriff. Nothing you can do about it now anyway."

"Lexa, please." His voice was softer now, the feral beast once again caged. "Tell me."

"A very bad man," I answered honestly.

"Give me a name, beautiful. Just his name and I'll make him pay for ever touching you."

I dropped my lashes, covering my eyes and hiding the pleasure I felt at his vow. "You can't. He's already dead." Pressing my lips into a hard line, I forced my lashes to lift and smiled coldly at him. "And that's all you'll ever get out of me on the subject, Sheriff Davis."

No way I would tell this man—the fucking law, for God's sake—that my mother killed the bastard who had nearly killed me.

TWO

I hated that cool little smile Lexa was giving me right then. It made me want to kiss her until she melted against me like she had the night before. I ached to feel her in my arms again, her mouth devouring mine just as hungrily as I would hers.

If she thought I couldn't see through it and glimpse the agonizing need that was burning through her—just as it was me—then I needed to set her straight. She'd put up walls since last night, and I was going to tear them down. Brick by brick if I had to.

"Here we go, Lexa," Quinn announced as she placed four, heavy-looking to-go bags on the counter. "I'll ring you up while Little John gets the sheriff's orders together."

Lexa gave her a forced smile. "Thanks, Aunt Quinn." As I watched, her tongue skimmed over her bottom lip, making it glossy, and I nearly released the groan that was vibrating in my throat. As she handed over a twenty for the first order, she bit into her bottom lip then blew out a small huff. "Hey, do you happen to know why Mom is taking the week off? They waited until the last minute to ask me to help out at the shop, and things seemed kind of tense this morning."

A frown squeezed at the blonde's brow as she handed over the change. "Sorry, honey. Things have been so crazy around here, I haven't really seen Raven in about a week. Although—" She broke off, shaking her head. "Never mind. I'm sure it's nothing. Your mom has been really busy lately. She probably just has to take care of other things, and with you home now, she can focus on them while you take care of the shop for her."

"Yeah," Lexa said with a nod, but I could tell she wasn't satisfied with that answer. Worry pinched at her brow before she quickly smoothed it out, putting on a smile that her aunt didn't seem to notice wasn't reaching her beautiful eyes.

Eight transactions later, and Lexa was finally ready to go. When she went to lift the bags, I was already there, taking two in each hand. "Lead the way," I instructed, only for her to glare up at me.

"I can carry it myself, Sheriff. I'm not helpless." Those glacier-blue eyes snapped icy fire at me, making the need to kiss her intensify. Did she have any idea how beautiful she was when she was pissed?

"No one thinks you are, woman. My grandmother would whup me good if I didn't offer some assistance." When she didn't move so I could follow her to her car, I turned and walked to the door alone.

I knew exactly which car was hers. When I'd pulled into the parking lot and saw it sitting close to the front door, my shitty morning at work had evaporated, and I'd felt a little of the peace I'd gotten a taste of the night before just looking at the stars with Lexa.

Turning so my back was to the door, I pushed it open with my shoulder and grinned at her. "Coming, beautiful?"

Muttering curses under her breath that would have had my grandmother swatting at her sexy behind, she stomped toward me and followed me out to her car. The doors weren't locked, so I secured the four bags in the back seat while she glowered at me. As I closed the door, she stepped back, crossing her arms over her chest mutinously, and I winked down at her before walking around to the driver's door and opening it for her.

"You can't do things like this and not expect people to notice," she said with a sexy little growl as she marched around the car toward me. "Especially here, of all places. Do you realize how many MC brothers eat here at any given time every single day?"

I shrugged. "I saw the cuts, sweetheart. I'm well aware of the club and its members." Leaning down, I brought my face to within an inch of hers. "Told you last night I don't care about them or your father."

"Yeah, well, I do." Tossing her hair out of her face, she showed me her scar for the third time since the night before. "Take a good look, Ben. It doesn't get any prettier in the sunlight."

Slamming the car door shut, I cupped her face in both hands, letting my thumb brush over her scar. "Stop it. I don't give a damn about this scar. It doesn't make you less beautiful to me, Lexa. It doesn't make me want you any less. I don't care about it or your father or anyone else in this goddamn world. I just want you to be mine."

Leaning into my touch, she lowered her lashes, but not before I saw the sheen of tears. Yet all too soon, she jerked back, putting distance between us all over again. "That didn't seem to be how you felt last night. I saw the disgust on your face, Sheriff. So, don't stand there and lie to me that you don't care about the fact that I'm—"

"Lexa?"

We both looked up at the sound of her name. When I saw the mountain of a man standing only feet away, his head shaved and a tattoo of a black widow on his neck, I instinctively put myself between him and Lexa. I knew who he was. No one would forget James Masterson after one introduction. The patch on his MC cut said Enforcer, and I could easily believe he would enforce every law his club had.

Noticing how protectively I was treating Lexa, he lifted his brows, but when he spoke, it wasn't to me. "Lexa, you okay here?"

Stepping around me, she walked over to him, not in the least bit intimidated by him. "Everything is fine, Uncle Spider." Standing on her tiptoes, she kissed his cheek. "Are you stopping for lunch?"

"Meeting Willa here," he told her, giving her a squeezing hug before releasing her and turning his menacing eyes back on me. "You got a problem with my niece, Sheriff?"

"Of course he doesn't," Lexa rushed to assure him without giving me time to speak. "He was nice enough to carry all my food out to my car for me."

"Why was he touching you, then?"

Because she's fucking mine, that's why.

But she didn't let me speak. "Because he saw my scar and was concerned. He wanted to know if I was okay and...who did this to me." She swallowed hard but put on a brave smile. "It seems our new sheriff wants justice for all his citizens."

"That right, Sheriff?" Masterson asked, skepticism thick in his voice.

Lexa turned her back to her uncle, her eyes pleading with me to agree with her. I couldn't deny her. "Yes, sir. Actually, I'd like to take the bastard who did this to her and give him my own form of justice."

His lips twitched, but he only nodded. "Wouldn't we all." Bending, he kissed the top of Lexa's head. "Glad you're home, sweetheart. Come by the house when you get the chance. We've all missed you."

"I'll do it soon," she promised as she faced him again. "I'm covering for Mom this week at the shop, though."

"Then I won't keep you. If you need anything, just let me know." He shot his eyes to me, drilling into me as if he could see everything as clear as day. "Sheriff," he half growled as he passed me.

"Masterson."

Lexa waited until the door to the diner closed behind him before letting out the breath she was holding. Glaring at me, she jerked open the driver's door. "You don't even know how close that was. Stay away from me, Ben. For your sake as well as mine, stay far, far away."

I caught the door before she could yank it closed and leaned in. She stopped pulling her seat belt across her chest, staring up at me in surprise.

"I can't stay away, beautiful. Can't—and won't." While she was still surprised, I kissed her quick. That small taste wasn't nearly enough, but I knew she was going to come to her senses soon, and I wouldn't put it past her to deck me. Pulling back just enough so our gazes locked, I stroked the backs of my fingers down her cheek. "Drive carefully."

Stepping back, I closed the door myself. Lexa stared at me for several long moments through her window, her mouth gaping open slightly. Then she seemed to shake herself out of the little daze I'd put her in and started her car. I waited until she'd pulled out of the parking lot before going inside for my staff's food orders.

As I walked up to the counter where Quinn was rearranging six large bags, I noticed Masterson sitting on one of the stools. Lifting his coffee, he took a large swallow, his eyes assessing me.

"I see you, Sheriff," he said in a low, deadly voice. "I see you."

"Good. Nice to know your eyes work, Masterson." Sliding my card across the counter to Quinn, I paid for all the food together.

"Stay away from Lexa."

"No," I told him point-blank. Not happening. She calmed the rage monster that not even the marines had completely tamed in all the years I'd served. I wasn't giving her up now that I had found her.

"Stay away from her, or this town will have to find a new sheriff." He said it casually, as if he were discussing the weather, but there was no mistaking the venom in his eyes, telling me without words there was nothing casual about what he was saying.

I didn't even blink at him. He probably scared the piss out of grown men on a daily basis with that deadly look in his eyes, but I wasn't shaking in my boots. No doubt he could bend a man like a pretzel with ease, but I hadn't survived the darkest bowels of hell without mastering a few skills of my own that would leave him crying for his mommy. "Threatening the law now?"

He shrugged. "I see it as more a warning. If you want to stay healthy, keep your hands to yourself."

Grabbing all six bags, I tipped my chin at him, grinning. "I'll be sure and keep that in mind." But my eyes were challenging him.

Bring it, motherfucker.

THREE

Ben's kiss still had me flustered as I locked up the shop at just after six that evening.

By the time I'd gotten back with everyone's food, I'd mostly snapped out of it, but the lingering tingle of my lips had distracted me as I'd dealt with customer after customer all afternoon. People had asked questions I couldn't remember if I even answered correctly because I was lost in my head, thinking about how good Ben's lips had felt against mine, how good that tiny taste of him had been.

Knowing I needed to pull myself together before I got home and my parents noticed my absent-mindedness, I mentally chastised myself as I walked toward my car.

"Night, Lexa," Trigger called as he put on his helmet and climbed onto his motorcycle. He was always the last to leave, and my car and his bike were the only two vehicles left in the parking lot. "Be careful driving home."

I smiled and waved as I climbed behind the wheel. "Night, Trigger."

He was already pulling out into traffic before I'd even started my car. Hitting the push-start so I could get the AC going, I took a moment to glance at my phone. I had a text from Mom telling me they were having pizza for dinner, so if I didn't want any, I needed to grab myself something on the way home. She knew I wasn't a fan of pizza after some kid at the local pizza place had been eating a freaking Snickers and then made our pizza when I was eight. That trip to the emergency room that night had aged Mom a good twenty years, and I'd avoided pizza ever since. So I decided to stop for a sandwich in town on my way home.

When I pulled up in front of Patty's Deli, the place was pretty deserted, but it was that way more often than not at dinnertime. Traffic down this street was always relatively sparse this time of the evening since all the other small businesses were already closed. Patty's wasn't as popular as Aggie's because she didn't have a large variety of things to choose from, but she made a killer sandwich and everything was allergen-friendly, so I tended to eat here more often than anywhere else.

But the best part of Patty's was the artwork she displayed from all the local artists. Once a week, she went to the elementary school and did art projects with each grade, and the best works from each class were always showcased in her front window. I couldn't remember how many times Mom would bring me here for a snack just so she could see my work in the window.

As I got out of my car, my eyes landed on the latest grade-school artwork, and I couldn't help but smile when I saw my cousin Nova's name on one of them. It was a painting of New York, her favorite place in the world and where she spent a few weeks every summer with her mom's family. She and her parents lived with mine, so I'd grown up listening to how much she missed New York from the time she got home until she left again the next summer. School would be out for the local kids by the end of the week, so I couldn't help but wonder when Nova and her brother would be leaving for their annual trip.

As I opened the door, a buzzer sounded, and Patty came out of the back with a rack loaded with freshly baked chocolate chip cookies. The heavenly smell had my stomach grumbling, reminding me I had barely touched my lunch earlier. My head had been so full of Ben, I hadn't even thought of food until the smells hit me.

"Well, if it isn't my best customer!" Patty greeted with a grin, placing the cookies on the counter and coming around to hug me. "How are you, sweetheart?"

I hugged her back. "Good. Busy, but good. How are you, Miss Patty?"

She sighed heavily and told me all about her oldest son marrying a girl from Washington she didn't care for. While she made my turkey and Swiss sandwich, she caught me up on all the local gossip, and I found the stress of the day slowly easing from my shoulders.

"Have you seen the new sheriff?" she asked as she packaged up three of the cookies for me, and all the tension returned to my body tenfold.

"We've met," I confirmed with a nod.

She waved her hand in front of her face, fanning herself. "Dear Lord, that boy," she laughed. Patty was in her late fifties, so to her, most men were boys. "And every single woman from the legal age of consent up to eighty is sniffing around that one. You wouldn't believe all the offers he's been getting since he came to town. And as soon as Sheriff Hogan stepped down, announcing Davis as his successor until the election this fall, it's only gotten worse. You would think this entire county was in heat the way those girls all throw themselves at the poor boy."

"Really?" I tried to act indifferent, when inside, I was suddenly fighting jealousy so intense, I wanted to scratch out the eyes of every female in the county who'd even looked twice at Ben. "I hadn't noticed anyone sniffing around, but I just met him."

"Next time you see him, watch. I bet you at least one local will try to get his attention in some shape or form. Especially over at Aggie's, from what I hear. That Tabby has made a fool of herself more than a few times, I've been told. Do you know how many flat tires he's had to change on the side of the road in the past month?" She laughed, shaking her head at how ridiculous it all was. "Why, just last week I saw him changing the tire for…"

Her voice trailed off when something out the front window caught her attention. Curious, I turned to follow her gaze, only to find the sheriff's cruiser had pulled up beside my car and Ben was getting out. The sun hadn't set yet, so I could see him perfectly. His gun was still attached to his belt, as was his flashlight, but he took the radio off and tossed it back inside the cruiser before shutting the door.

Pushing his sunglasses up on his head, he looked in and caught my gaze, and my lips started to tingle all over again from his kiss that afternoon. As I stood there watching, he walked into the deli.

"Good evening, Sheriff. What can I do for you?" Patty asked as she bagged up all of my food.

"Miss Patty," he said with a smile that nearly knocked me on my ass then and there, and that was before he turned it on me. Once he did, I had to grasp hold of the counter to steady myself. "I'll take whatever she's having."

"Of course. Exactly the same?"

"Please." Crossing to stand beside me, he brushed his upper arm against my chest, and I couldn't help the sharp inhale as my nipples hardened at the deceptively innocent touch. That wicked smile he gave me said he knew exactly what he was doing to me.

I had to get out of there before I did something I would regret. I was weak where this man was concerned. Weak and stupid. Earlier, I'd allowed him to kiss me even though Uncle Spider had been right inside Aggie's. Uncle Spider was just as dangerous as Dad. He wouldn't hesitate to hurt or even kill Ben if given a reason. And I wouldn't be the reason something happened to the man I was crazily starting to care about.

"How much do I owe you, Miss Patty?" I got out in a weak voice.

"I got this," Ben informed me. "Then we could go to the park and eat if you want. I'm off duty now."

"No." Definitely no. I couldn't be alone with him again like we were the night before. Ten minutes with no one around, not even a single car, and I'd been ready to let him take me against the hood of my freaking car.

Taking a ten out of my wallet, I placed it on the counter, not even caring about the change.

But no sooner did it touch the surface than he picked it up and pushed it back into my hand. "Don't argue with me about this," he said, narrowing his eyes. "I'm paying for dinner."

"Sheriff," I half growled in frustration, my hand burning from his touch where he was still cupping the money in my palm.

"Lexa," he countered.

From the other side of the counter, Patty tried to stifle her laugh, and my face heated. Fuck. This was going to be all over town before the end of the night.

I was reminded of the gossip Patty told me earlier, and all thoughts of my parents finding out about this disappeared, replaced once again with jealousy. Crumpling the money in my fist, I lifted my brows at Ben. "You go around buying dinner for every girl, Sheriff?"

"Do my grandmother and secretary count as girls?" he asked, amusement in his eyes. He knew I was jealous, and it was funny to him. "Because I bought my sixty-year-old secretary lunch today."

"What about all the girls whose tires you change?" I demanded, so mad now, I was shaking. But the thought of Ben screwing his way through Trinity County's single female population hurt more than I ever could have imagined it would. "You buy them a meal after? Take them back to your place for a picnic in bed?"

The amusement died a quick death in his eyes, and he lost his smile. "What are you talking about, woman? What did I miss?"

"Nothing," I bit out. "Thanks for the sandwich and cookies." Glancing at Patty, who was eating up every moment of our exchange, I forced a smile. "See you next time, Miss Patty."

"Sure thing, hon. Tell your mom I said hi."

Bag in hand, I stomped out of the deli and was at my car before Ben caught up with me. "Lexa, what just happened back there?" he demanded, catching my car door in his hands as I flung it open and tossed everything into the passenger seat.

Before I could get in, he was around the door and grasping hold of my arm in a firm enough grip to hold me in place without hurting me. "Hey, talk to me, baby. I feel like I'm walking in an active minefield right now, and trust me, I know from experience that isn't fun."

"I'm not joining the Ben Davis fan club," I told him point-blank, glaring up into his handsome face. "Apparently, it already has plenty of members, so you don't need one more." Jerking my arm free, I got into my car.

"What fan club? For fuck's sake, Lexa, what the hell are you talking about?" he demanded, so frustrated, he scrubbed his hands over his face. "Why are you so mad at me?"

"How many times have you hooked up since coming to town, Ben?" I whisper-shouted.

His jaw turned to stone. "Why does that matter?"

"It just does!"

Scratching at the scruff on his jaw, he groaned. "I don't know. A few, maybe. That was before I became sheriff, though. It was before I met *you*. Not one of them lasted longer than a few nights."

"Just like I won't last more than a few nights," I concluded. My heart started to throb in my chest, and my eyes stung with tears I wasn't going to let spill free.

"No!" He exploded. "How did we go from me buying you dinner, to you accusing me of sleeping with all the people I've changed tires for, to you thinking we wouldn't last?"

"It's a logical chain of thought to reach the right conclusion. I'm not like everyone else. I'm not going to hop into bed with you just because you bought me dinner."

"I didn't expect you to." Crouching down, he took my hand and brought it to his lips, kissing my palm. "Miss Patty was telling you the gossip, am I right?" Something in my eyes must have told him just how right he was. "I've changed a few tires for women, Lexa. But not nearly as many as everyone says I have. And honestly, I don't know how changing tires for women who don't even carry around a jack went straight to me taking them to bed. I'm the sheriff. It's my responsibility to help anyone in need. I haven't slept with any of them, though. I swear to you."

His tongue touched the center of my palm, and I felt myself melting. The raging jealousy that was making me see red and unable to think straight started to clear, and I realized I'd just acted like a crazy girlfriend. But I couldn't ever be Ben's girlfriend, even if I wanted it more than anything.

"I believe you," I told him, knowing I should pull my hand free but unable to bring myself to do so.

Relief filled his eyes. "Let me go get my food and pay, and we can go somewhere and talk."

"I can't. My parents are expecting me." Reluctantly, I pulled away, already missing his touch, his lips on my skin. "I have to go."

"Okay. I'm not going to make you." His huge left hand touched my thigh. "Give me your number so I can call you later."

"Ben, we can't do this." And I needed to remind myself of all the reasons why we couldn't do this. Whatever the hell "this" was.

"Lexa, I need to hear your voice before I go to sleep tonight." His fingers caressed up my thigh before slowly moving back down. I moaned at how much I wanted him to go higher, but his hand stayed where it was. "Or I'm going to show up at your house and climb the drainpipe and sneak in to your room. Then I'm going to have to arrest myself for breaking and entering. You don't want that, do you, baby?"

Gulping, I grabbed the pen out of the cupholder and turned his hand over. I believed he would do it. But worse than that, part of me wanted him to sneak in to my bedroom. And do so many naughty things to me.

My fingers shook as I wrote my number on his palm. "I really have to go now."

"Okay. Drive carefully." His thumb brushed over my inner thigh and, even through my jeans, my skin felt scorched.

"Thanks again for dinner," I told him as he straightened and stepped back.

"Hopefully next time, we can eat together." Winking down at me, he shut the door.

As I backed out of the parking space, he lifted his hand, his gaze following me hungrily. Biting my lip, I waved back.

No matter how much I told him and myself that this thing between us couldn't go anywhere, that it was dangerous, I kept falling deeper and deeper into the pit and giving in a little more every time I saw him.

I was totally fucked, and if I wasn't careful, it was going to get him killed.

FOUR

The house was loud when I got home. Walking into the kitchen, I found Mom sitting at the table with Aunt Flick and Aunt Willa, the sound of Aunt Willa's kids screaming and laughing from the living room with Nova and Garret filling the entire house.

The three women at the table couldn't have been more different in looks. Mom was tall and willowy with blond hair. In the Angel's Halo MC, she was the queen, and everyone respected her. From the other ol' ladies to the sheep who practically lived at the clubhouse, the females associated with the MC knew that Raven

Hannigan Reid ruled and her husband, the president, jumped to do her bidding.

Aunt Flick was the curviest of the three, her hair no longer holding the bright red dye she'd once worn when I was a kid, now its natural, pretty shade of brown instead. She was also the calmest one of the three, the nurturer when needed. Years before when she'd gone into preterm labor with Nova, we'd all been scared we were going to lose her. That was the second time I'd seen my mother cry, the first being when I'd gotten my scar. Thankfully for us all, both Aunt Flick and Nova had been too stubborn to leave us.

But it was my aunt Willa, the only one at the table I actually shared DNA with, who was an enigma to me. For the first few years of my life, after my biological mother died, she and my dad raised me in Washington. She potty trained me, helped Dad through that first scary realization that I had a life-threatening food allergy. But when Dad and Mom got back together and I became Mom's shadow, Willa had stepped back to let us build our bond. Since then, I'd lost some of our connection, but we were both okay with that. She knew that I needed Mom and her triplets needed her.

She was married to the second scariest member of the MC, and everyone was amused by how tiny little Willa could so easily get the badass known as Spider Masterson to do her bidding with just a pout of her lips. But what really got me was how his daughters could manipulate him so easily. Especially Mila. Monroe was the quiet, sweet twin, but Mila was sly as a fox.

Like it had that morning when I'd come downstairs, the conversation stopped as soon as I walked into the kitchen, putting me on edge all over again.

I dropped my bag on the table in front of them and glared down at all three women. "Okay, I'm tired of this already. Something is going on, and I want to know what it is right now."

They all shared a look, contemplating whether or not to tell me, and a ball of dread filled my stomach. No way was I going to be able to eat now.

"Maybe you should just tell her, Rave," Aunt Flick urged softly. "You're going to have to sooner or later."

When Mom's chin started to tremble, my knees went weak. Holding on to the back of the chair for support, I kept my gaze glued on her as she closed her eyes and finally nodded. "Sit down, baby."

"Just say it," I whispered, unable to move for fear of my legs finally giving out.

"Today…your dad took me for some tests." Tears filled her eyes, and she blinked rapidly, trying to keep them contained.

"What kinds of tests?" I was able to choke out, my voice shaking as badly as my knees.

"I-I had my pap smear last week, and the results came back. It wasn't good. The doctor suspects…"

I was going to be sick. Before she even said the words I realized were coming from just the look on her face, I knew I was going to throw up.

"She thinks I have cervical cancer."

I made it to the sink before the bile left my mouth. Aunt Flick was there, rubbing my back as I sobbed while still retching. Then I felt Mom's touch, and the tears started pouring out of my eyes uncontrollably.

Stroking my hair back from my face, she pressed her forehead to my shoulder. "Shh, shh. It's okay."

How could she say that to me? She was the one who was sick, the one who could fucking die. But she was trying to soothe me. The one person I loved more than life itself might be stolen from me, and I didn't know if I could take it.

"We don't even know if that's what this is or not." She tried to reassure me, but her voice was raspy, and I suspected she didn't believe what she was saying. "Th-that's why I went in for more tests today. It could just be…"

"Mom." Wiping my mouth with the wet paper towel Aunt Willa offered, I turned so I was facing Mom, and I was startled to realize she'd changed in the months since I'd been away at college.

Why hadn't I noticed before now? I'd only been home for a few days, but I still should have noticed that she'd lost weight. And Mom was so thin to begin with, she didn't have anything to lose. There were dark circles under her green eyes. She looked small and fragile, and that was one word I never thought I would associate with my mom.

"Do you think this is cancer?"

She wasn't quick enough to mask the truth that flashed across her eyes, and I was glad I'd just thrown up everything in my stomach or I would have been vomiting all over again. "Yes," she said after a moment. "I avoided going for my yearly exam for years, and only went when I started having issues. I knew before I even went that something was wrong."

"How bad…is it?"

She sighed so heavily, her shoulders shook. "I won't know until the tests from today come back. But the doctor is rushing everything because she thinks it's already pretty advanced from all the symptoms I'd told her about."

Oh God. "Mom," I whispered. "I don't… I can't…"

Two tears spilled over her lashes as she lost the battle to hold them back. "I know. Lexa, I know." She pulled me into her arms for a tight hug, rocking me like she used to when I was a little girl. "The good news is that it's treatable. Dad and I have already talked about the options, and we'll do whatever the doctor suggests. A hysterectomy, chemotherapy. Whatever is needed."

That didn't make me feel any better about any of this. Chemotherapy would make her sick. One of my teachers in high school had been diagnosed with breast cancer, and the chemo treatments had

SALVATION: ANGEL'S HALO NEXT GEN

made her so sick, she'd eventually quit her job because she could barely stand. Even with the treatment and having a double mastectomy, she'd died a year later.

I couldn't lose Mom. She was everything to me and to so many other people. She kept us all glued together. Without her, our family would completely fall apart.

Mom cleared her throat. "Listen, Lexa. I don't want you to tell your brother or your uncles about this. Jet knows, and so does Spider. But the others don't. I want to wait until we have all the results back before we tell everyone else. Okay?"

Scrubbing my hands over my face, I pulled away from her enough to nod. "Yeah. I won't tell anyone. I promise."

***

My eyes felt swollen but oddly dry as I climbed into bed an hour later. It was still fairly early, but I couldn't be around the others tonight and not cry.

I couldn't just sit around and do nothing, though. I needed to make plans. Mom was sick, and there was no damn way I was just going to leave again at the end of the summer. Anonymity at Oregon had been nice, but I was needed at home.

Getting my laptop out of my backpack, I enrolled online at the local university to start the ball rolling. Mom had been dropping hints she wanted me to move back home for months, but I knew she wouldn't let me quit college. She hadn't gone herself, but she wanted me to.

After taking care of that, I started searching for all the information I could on cervical cancer and its treatment.

I was neck-deep in WebMD hell when my phone rang. Still reading, despite my vision going blurry from my latest fight with tears from what I was taking in, I lifted my phone without looking away from the computer screen. "Hello?" I rasped out, sniffling before wiping my nose on one of the many tissues already crumpled around me.

"Lexa?" Ben's voice was all growly, and oddly, the sound of it eased some of the pressure around my heart I'd been feeling since Mom dropped her bombshell on me.

"H-hey," I hiccupped. "Hold on a sec, okay?" Without waiting for him to reply, I dropped the phone on the bed beside me and grabbed a fresh tissue to blow my nose.

When I picked it up again, he was already talking. "Did you make it home okay?"

"I'm home." Closing my laptop, I pushed it to the foot of the bed, then fell back against my pillows. Grabbing the extra one, I pulled it to my chest and hugged it as tight as I could.

"What's wrong, baby?"

Closing my eyes, I wanted to tell him everything, but I'd promised Mom I wouldn't tell anyone. Ben was an outsider, so I couldn't tell him even if she hadn't asked me not to. "Just family drama," I told him instead, and the ache around my heart intensified.

"Lexa," he groaned. "I wish you would tell me. I can hear how upset you are in your voice, beautiful."

"I…can't," I told him honestly. "My mom asked me not to tell anyone, and I'd never break a promise to her."

"Yeah, okay. I get it." He blew out a tired sigh. "Whatever it is, though, I'm here if you need me."

Tears fell from my eyes again, and I scrubbed at them. "Thank you," I whispered.

"I wish I was there so I could hold you."

Me too.

Clearing my throat, I changed the subject. "What are you doing right now?"

"Sitting in my living room, missing you."

"You just saw me two hours ago," I reminded him, a smile teasing at my lips despite all the pressure trying to cave in my chest.

"I started missing you as soon as your car backed away from the deli earlier." I heard him shifting and then swallowing, and I imagined him with his feet up on a coffee table, a beer in his hand...

His shirt off and in nothing more than a pair of boxers with his hair wet from a shower.

Need burned through me at the mental picture I was creating, and I had to squeeze my thighs together to alleviate some of the tension building there.

When I opened my eyes again, I glanced down at the ragged old T-shirt and sweats I'd changed into after my own shower earlier. There was nothing exciting or the least bit sexy about my typical pajamas, and I wanted to be both those things for him.

"Beautiful? You still there?"

"Yeah, sorry." I kicked off my sweats, but I still didn't feel any better. If anything, the ache between my legs only intensified. "Just trying to get comfortable."

"Oh yeah?" His voice dropped, getting deeper and husky, making me shiver. "How?"

"I just kicked off my sweat pants." I heard him groan, which made me laugh softly. "Don't get too excited. I still have on my ratty old T-shirt I've had since I was, like, thirteen."

"I need to give you a new one, then. One of mine. Yeah, I like that idea. I'll bring you one tomorrow," he promised.

A knock on my door had me jerking upright. From the heaviness of it, I knew it was most likely my dad. I glanced down at my phone, guilt pouring over me like a bucket of ice water. "Lexa?" Dad called through the door. "You got a minute?"

"Yeah, Dad. Just a sec." Lifting the phone to my ear, I grabbed my sweats and pulled them back on one-handed. "I have to go," I whispered. "Don't call back."

"Lex—"

I hung up before he could even finish my name and cleared his number from my phone in a moment of paranoia. Dad wouldn't look at my phone, but I wasn't going to take any chances. I'd loved talking to Ben, but even that much contact with him was risky.

Hiding my phone under my pillow, I jumped out of bed and ran to the door. Opening it, I faced Dad. There was a hint of tequila on his breath, telling me he'd been at Hannigans' all evening. After what Mom confessed to me earlier, I didn't blame him for needing a drink. I kind of needed one too.

His eyes, so like my own, scanned over me as if he expected to find something wrong with me. And maybe they were a little suspicious, but that particular emotion was gone so quickly, I was sure I had imagined it.

I could only imagine how I looked. My cheeks felt hot with the shame that was trying to consume me. I felt like a fucking traitor.

"Everything okay, sweetheart?" he asked, his voice soft and concerned.

"Y-yeah," I lied, nodding. "It's just…everything."

Ice-blue eyes darkened with pain. "Can I come in for a minute?"

I stepped back, letting him enter my bedroom. When he walked over to my window, I shut the door and turned to face him, waiting.

"Mom said she told you. How are you taking it?"

I wrapped my arms around myself, mentally telling myself not to cry. "I don't want to believe it. Is there a scarier word than 'cancer'? Because I'll be honest with you, Dad, I'm terrified right now."

He clenched his jaw, and I saw his throat work a few times before he finally nodded. "I know, Lexa. I'm pretty scared myself. Your mom is…everything to me. But we're going to fight this. You don't have to worry. We're not going to lose her."

"You can't know that for sure," I whispered. "You're not God."

"No, but I know Raven, and I know that she is nothing if not a fighter. No matter what happens, she's going to fight this until her last breath. She won't give up. That's how I know we won't lose her."

The strength and conviction in his voice gave me hope. Maybe we wouldn't lose Mom to this damned disease. I started to relax a little, some of the strain over Mom's illness leaving my muscles.

"Spider mentioned something to me this evening."

Oh fuck. Here it comes.

"About?" I asked, trying to keep my voice casual, while inside, I was a quaking mess. I could feel a change in the air of the room. It felt charged and dangerous, and I didn't know how to react to that. I knew Dad would never hurt me, but that wasn't what I was worried about.

"Is the new sheriff giving you a problem, Lexa?" he demanded, crossing his arms over his massive chest, the softness leaving his voice.

"No, of course not," I half exclaimed. "Why would you think that?"

"Because Spider said he walked up on the two of you in Aggie's parking lot, and you were upset about something. He told me fucking Davis had his hands on you." He was seething now, and my heart started pounding. "Now, tell me honestly. Was he giving you a hard time?"

"No! He carried the food to my car. That's all."

"Lexa, don't lie to me," he bellowed, and I couldn't help but flinch. He didn't yell at me like that. My brother, sure. Max was always getting into trouble. But never me. "If he didn't have an issue with you, then something is going on between you two. Gracie called Hawk at the bar and said she heard he bought you dinner tonight at Patty's. So, I'm going to give you one more chance here, little girl. What is going on with you and the sheriff?"

Panic tried to choke me, but I fought it down. "Nothing!" I cried. "He wants there to be something, but I told him no. Repeatedly. I'm not an idiot! He's a cop. The damn sheriff, for fuck's sake. I know nothing can happen between him and me."

"You're damn right. He's just trying to use you to find out shit on us. What if he's looking into your mother? She told you about Fontana against my wishes because she thought it would help you after what happened. She didn't want you to be scared anymore, Lexa. Now, suddenly, the sheriff is sniffing around you, when I know for a fact that motherfucker has plenty of pussy all lined up for him."

I couldn't help flinching at that mental picture he was painting for me. Was he right? Could Ben just be after an in to find something on my family? Was he using me?

I wanted to say no, he would never do something like that to me. But my head couldn't help but wonder if it was true. It made sense. Why else would someone who looked like him want someone who looked like me?

"Everyone in this town knows how tight you and your mom are. All it would take is one whisper of a hint that she took out Fontana to save you, and they could link it to the MC and invoke RICO like the damn district attorney has wanted to do for decades. I don't care about me, but do you really want to put her at risk? Especially right now?" He raked his hands through his hair, a sign of angry frustration I couldn't remember him using while dealing with me, and I understood his reaction to this a little better.

He was more worried about Mom than he was letting on, and he was taking it out on me. His stress levels must have been off the charts with fear for her, and I was getting the brunt of it.

But it still stung.

"She has enough shit going on right now not to have to deal with you fucking around with the goddamn law, Lexa. This will only stress her out more."

"I-I'm sorry. It won't happen again," I promised, blinking back tears.

His face only tightened even more, his eyes seeming to flash with lightning at me. "Keep him away, Lexa. Or I'll take care of him myself. Do you hear me?"

"Yes, Dad," I told him quietly. "I hear you."

FIVE

Paperwork was the bane of my existence, it seemed. I had a mountain of it on my desk every morning when I walked into my office, and this morning was no different.

What was different was the district attorney sitting in front of said desk, strumming his fingers on the chair's arms impatiently as I entered. Of all the things I disliked about being sheriff—and there really weren't many—having to deal with this slimy sonofabitch was the one I hated the most.

Mayor Jenkins and I agreed on the DA wholeheartedly, but for some damn reason, the citizens continued to reelect Royce Campbell. He took half a term off to run for mayor from what I'd heard, but when Jenkins won the special election, Campbell had licked his wounds and run for DA once again, sweeping the rug out from under his appointed replacement at the time.

Something suspicious was going on with that, but I didn't have cause to investigate it. And even if I did, I would have to bring in the state's attorney general, and I just wasn't ready to deal with that drama. Yet. If the bastard ever gave me a reason, though, I'd put his neck on a chopping block.

"Sheriff," Campbell greeted as he stood, his hand already extended for me to shake.

Out of professional courtesy, I did, but I kept it brief before dropping my hand and walking around my desk to take my seat. "What brings you in, Campbell?"

"You, actually." He retook his own seat without being invited to. Leaning forward eagerly, he grinned so broadly I felt dirty just being in the same room with him. I would put him close to sixty, but the world wouldn't know that from his dyed hair and his smooth face from all the Botox Gran said the man got on the regular. "Word around town is you and Lexa Reid are becoming

Creswell Springs' favorite couple in their daily soap opera."

Her name coming off his tongue made me want to put my fist through his face. Instead, I didn't show an ounce of emotion, knowing that was exactly what he wanted. "And where did you hear that?"

"The more appropriate question is, where haven't I heard it?" he said with a sly laugh. "If I'd known you were going to dick around with Reid's daughter, of all people, I would have been in here a hell of a lot sooner. So, tell me your plan. How long are you planning to string this girl along until she spills a few MC secrets? Her mother is her best friend, so I know the girl has to be privy to a few juicy details that we can use to put those bastards behind bars where they really belong."

I sat up straighter in my chair, my dislike only growing for this worthless man the longer he sat there gleefully waiting for me to answer.

"First, she's a woman, not a girl. Second, my relationship with Lexa Reid is none of your fucking business. And third, I don't have a plan now, nor will I ever use what she knows about her family against her or them." I stood and pressed my palms flat on the desktop as I leaned forward to glare at him.

Right then, that desk was the only protection Campbell had against me, and if he knew any better, he would make a run for it. The rage I'd always struggled to contain was just below the surface, and if he kept running his mouth, I was going to destroy him and make him eat all the words he was spewing about Lexa.

"All we need is one felony, and we can charge them all. Bring the Feds in and invoke RICO. We can get rid of the entire lot of them and clean up this town once and for all," Campbell continued. "You'll be a hero to this town, Davis. Just what you need to get reelected come fall."

A hero?

Bullshit. From what I'd seen of the citizens in and around Creswell Springs, they loved the MC. Respected them. Crime was low, and I wasn't stupid enough to think it was because of me. Whatever the MC did when they were out of town, they never brought it back with them, and they kept the rougher crowd that lived within Trinity County in check, with the exception of the college assholes who didn't know any better.

No one complained about the MC—at least, they hadn't to me. Even my grandparents seemed to like them. My grandmother, who had an opinion on everyone, didn't have a bad one of the motorcycle club as far as I knew.

I didn't need to be a hero to get reelected. No one wanted the job, and so far, no one had voiced the possibility of running against me. That was, if I decided to run. I hadn't made up my mind yet, but Sheriff Hogan, Mayor Jenkins, and both my grandparents were all pushing for it.

"Why do you want them gone so bad?" I asked, curious enough about his motives to see through the red haze covering my eyes and hold off killing him for the moment.

"If I were you, I would be worried about yourself and want them gone too. Sheriff Bates, who was sheriff before Hogan, disappeared under mysterious circumstances and was never seen or heard from again. The last time his neighbors saw him, Raven Reid was breaking in to his house, and then she and Sebastian Reid put him in their car and drove him away. Hogan was untouchable to them because he was buddies with Jenkins. But, you? You're dicking around with the MC president's only daughter. Pretty sure that puts you at the top of their hit list."

Standing, Campbell smirked. "Wouldn't want you to disappear on us, boy. The citizens of this county like you, and your grandparents would be beside themselves with grief and worry. You're their last remaining family, from what I hear."

As the door shut behind him, I heard him laugh, and I picked up my chair, ready to throw it. But before I could toss it, the door opened and in walked the mayor, a thunderous look on his weathered face.

Once he took note of the look on my face, some of his own anger subsided, and he shut and locked the door before walking across to take the same chair Campbell had just vacated.

"Put the office furniture down, son. No need in destroying the place. The bastard is gone." Crossing his legs, he leaned back in the chair, seeming to get comfortable as I slowly placed my own chair back on the floor and dropped down into it.

Scrubbing my hands over my face, I swallowed the bellow that was trapped in my throat but I refused to release.

"Why did I get a call at the ass-crack of dawn telling me to keep my sheriff away from Bash Reid's daughter?" he demanded after a pause, giving me a little extra time to calm down.

I snapped my head up. "Who was the caller?"

"Bash Reid himself. We go way back, as I'm sure you know. I was the club's defense attorney for decades. But he doesn't come making demands of me at random. And believe me, this was very much a demand. Then, when I stopped for coffee at Aggie's this morning, it was to walk into everyone talking about our beloved sheriff playing around with the MC's princess."

"Shit," I groaned. Everyone talking of our potential relationship was only going to make Lexa that much more skittish.

"It seems there was a heated debate taking place on whether you were genuine in your pursuit of young Lexa or if you were scheming with Campbell to get as much dirt on the club as possible before arresting someone." He nodded toward the closed door. "Then I walk into the station to find that slimy piece of donkey shit leaving your office. You can imagine what I was thinking until I walked in here and found you ready to destroy a considerably pricey desk chair."

I didn't care what he thought I was doing. I was stuck on the fact that some people actually thought I would use Lexa to get to her father. Bash Reid, or any other MC member, wasn't even on the radar.

Ah fuck, did Lexa think I was using her?

Grabbing my phone off the desk where I'd tossed it, I called her. But there was no answer. Muttering curses, I shot her a text, only to have it kicked back, saying it was unable to be delivered.

"Goddamn it!" I threw the phone back on the desk. The thing was useless to me now because Lexa had blocked me.

I was starting to shake, could feel the rage taking over, and fuck if I knew how to control it.

With a roar, I swept my arms over the top of the desk, sending paperwork and my computer monitor crashing to the floor so hard that the sound of the monitor's screen cracking echoed throughout the room.

"Hey, take it easy there, boy," Jenkins said as he got nervously to his feet.

Jumping up, I grabbed my keys and nearly ripped the door off its hinges as I stormed out, hearing the mayor call after me.

Nothing he said right then mattered. I needed to get to Lexa and reassure her that I wasn't using her.

I drove by her house just to see if she'd left for work yet, and her car was already gone. Hitting the gas, I headed for her father's garage. My brakes screamed I slammed them so hard as I pulled up in front of the shop.

A dull buzzer sounded as I opened the door. Lexa was behind the counter, dressed in a black polo with the garage's logo on the left breast and tan shorts, her hair down and covering the right side of her face as it always was. Five people stood around waiting to be dealt with while she tended to the customer in front of her. But all eyes were on me, surprise and curiosity on every face except for Lexa's.

Her face was set in angry lines, but it was the pain in her beautiful, glacier-blue eyes that nearly brought me to my knees.

"Baby—"

"I'm busy here, Sheriff," she interrupted, her tone hard and icy. "If you need your vehicle worked on or to order a part, stand in line and wait your turn. I'll be with you as soon as I can. Otherwise, please don't loiter in the shop."

"Oh, he can go ahead of me," the guy at the counter said with a grin as he stepped back. "Wouldn't want to risk the safety of the town if Sheriff Davis gets an emergency call."

"You have such a kind soul, Higgins," she said dryly.

"Anything for you, Lexa babe." He scanned his eyes over her, and some of the haze that had started to lift at the sight of the only person to ever calm me returned. I looked the guy over, noticing he was Lexa's age, maybe a little older. He looked at her like he wanted to devour her whole, and I stepped toward him menacingly.

Lexa came around the counter and pushed at my chest. The feel of her hands on me stopped me in my tracks, doing what her strength alone couldn't. I covered them, pressing them harder against my heart as I looked down at her with pleading eyes.

"Outside," she commanded and pushed again, but still, I was unmovable.

Keeping one of her hands in mine, I followed her out to my vehicle. The monster inside me was completely calm now, and I finally felt like I could breathe again.

Able to think clearly, I felt eyes on us and turned to find all the customers, including Higgins, standing at the window looking out. But there were others watching now as well. Bash Reid stood there with eyes that were just as hard as his daughter's had been when I first walked into the shop. His huge, inked arms were crossed over his chest as he just stood there watching us.

Lexa glanced back too, and I felt her tremble when her gaze landed on her father. Jerking her hand out of my hold, she put distance between us before facing me. "You need to leave. Right now."

"Not until you hear me out. Lexa, I swear—"

"No!" she cried, tears filling her eyes, tearing me apart inside. "I can't do this with you. I've told you so many times I've lost count, and yet I kept giving in. Apparently, I'm weak whenever you're around, but that stops now. I have too much shit going on in my life at the moment to constantly have to wonder if the guy I care about is going to use something I say inadvertently against the people I love."

"I would never do that to you. Your family doesn't matter to me, I've told you that just as many times." Erasing the distance between us, I cupped both sides of her face in my hands. "Just give me a chance."

"You're asking too much. I refuse to let anything touch my family, including you." A tear fell from her eyes, making it impossible to breathe for a moment. "Stay away from me, Ben."

"Lexa—"

"She said to stay away, Sheriff," Bash said behind me in a hard voice. "Now get your fucking hands off her. You might be the law in this town, but you touch my daughter again, and Campbell will need to find a new little bitch to do his dirty work."

I dropped my hands and clenched them into fists. Lexa's trembling only intensified, but the tears in her eyes dried up in the next heartbeat. Her gaze stayed locked on mine, seeming to plead with me not to argue, telling me so much that I couldn't decipher.

"Please go," she whispered. "Don't argue with him. It will only make this worse."

"Meet me tonight," I mouthed, and her eyes locked on to my lips.

Her lashes lowered, but I got the answer I wanted before I finally stepped back from her. Turning to walk to my car, I tipped up my chin at Bash along the way.

"You have a good day, Sheriff," he said with a snarl on his face. "Stay safe."

Clenching my fists, I reminded myself not to do anything reckless. I could handle him with no problem, but if I punched her father, it wouldn't win me any points with him. "I'll be seeing you, Reid," I told him as I climbed behind the wheel of my cruiser.

As I pulled out of the parking lot, my eyes went back to Lexa. She stood there watching me go, her face blank as her father spoke to her. Before she faded from my view, I watched him hug her, and I clenched my hands around the wheel.

Gritting my teeth, I knew there was only one way to deal with this shit. By the time I got back to the station and walked into the disaster I'd left of my office, I had a plan. Slamming the door shut, I found my phone in the wreckage of the scattered papers and broken screen of my computer.

Dropping down into my chair, I pulled up the contact I needed just as my secretary walked in, caution masking her face. Margaret was a little younger than my grandmother, her hair short, gray, and permed on the regular. She was also my grandmother's closest friend, so I knew without a doubt, Gran either already knew about this morning's events or would very soon.

"How about a cup of coffee?" she offered hesitantly.

"Sounds good," I told her as I hit connect on the number on my phone. "Then don't let anyone bother me for a few hours. I've got work to do." As she nodded, I got an answer and leaned my head back against the chair, closing my eyes as I spoke to the woman on the other end. "Paige, how are you?"

"What do you want, Ben?" she asked, sounding exasperated, but I could also hear the huskiness in her voice. That same huskiness she used to try to get me to do whatever the hell she wanted. But Paige never had the hold over me she thought she did.

Not like Lexa did.

"You know that favor I've been holding on to for the last five years?" I heard her grunt, the noise anything but ladylike.

That more than anything told me how affected she was by my sudden call. Paige Stanford was always the perfect lady. No hair out of place, not so much as a speck of lint or a single wrinkle on her dresses. We'd dated for all of two minutes before I'd started losing my damn mind when she tried to change me.

But she still owed me a favor, and her father was the state's attorney general.

And I needed Campbell out of my hair once and for all.

Lexa's dad thought I was working with the bastard, and the slimy DA was trying to make it look like I was to everyone. I'd be damned if that motherfucker would be the reason Lexa was taken from me. He had to go, sooner rather than later.

"Yes, I remember," she grumbled. "What's it going to cost me?"

"Depends on how you look at it. Make this happen for me, and we could even say I owe you one." I gritted my teeth, already wondering if I was selling my soul.

With Paige, it was anyone's guess.

SIX

"Where you going, honey?"

I stopped in my tracks on the way to the back door. Slowly, I turned to face Mom, who was sitting at the kitchen table with Dad and Aunt Flick. Cups of coffee sat in front of them all, and huge slices of cheesecake had been placed on the table for the two women that I was surprised were untouched. Cheesecake didn't last long when it came to Mom and Aunt Flick. It was one of their comfort foods.

"I was going to go to the library and get some reading done," I told her, lifting the books in my arms to show her. "I couldn't concentrate with

Max, Reid, and Garret playing video games so loudly upstairs."

"Well, don't be out late," Mom said, sipping her coffee.

"I won't," I promised, moving toward the door once more and doing my best to avoid Dad's gaze.

"Lexa, could I ask a favor?" Aunt Flick asked before I could reach my destination.

Shifting the books in my arms, I turned to face her. "Sure, if I can help, I will."

"Nova and Garret are going to New York tomorrow, and I was wondering if you could fly out with them, make sure they get to Ciro and Scarlett's. It will only be overnight. The Vitucci jet will bring you back the next day." She pushed her uneaten cheesecake away, and I knew she was beyond upset about something. "Normally, I would go, but something came up and I can't. But if I cancel, Nova will lose her damn mind, and I really can't deal with that shit right now."

I nearly groaned. What she meant was she needed me to watch Garret and make sure he didn't set the Vituccis' private jet on fire or drive the pilot and other crew so crazy they decide to crash to put themselves—and the world in general—out of their misery. Nova could have made the flight on her own given the number of guards Ciro sent to accompany his cousin's children to New York to ensure their safety. But it was more than likely that Garret would cause pure carnage if not kept in constant check.

"But what about the shop?" I hedged.

"I'm going to work at the shop tomorrow, honey. There are a lot of things I need to make sure are taken care of before I start treatment, and I'd feel better if I took care of them now, rather than leave you in the lurch later on while I'm down and out," Mom assured me. "We would both really appreciate it if you could go with the kids. Garret doesn't listen to anyone else but me, Flick, and you. It would really be helping us all out."

Pressing my lips together, I gave in. "What time do we leave tomorrow?"

"You will need to leave here by six in the morning. Just pack a small carry-on, enough for a few days," Aunt Flick said, her eyes full of thanks.

"But you just said it was only overnight," I corrected her.

She shrugged. "Who knows, maybe you'll want to go shopping. Theo Volkov wouldn't mind spending time with you, I'm sure."

My eyes narrowed on her and then my parents, but if I called them out on what I suspected, I knew it would only cause more trouble for me. My guess was Dad—or any number of gossip gremlins—already told Mom about Ben and me, and they wanted me as far away from Creswell Springs as possible.

"I'm leaving," I told them, opening the back door.

"Don't be late," Mom called after me. "You still need to pack."

"Yeah, yeah," I muttered to myself as I slammed the door and practically sprinted to my car.

The sun was going down as I drove through town and parked at the library. It was in the middle of town, and anyone coming from the police station would have to drive by it. I parked right on the street out front and walked in, waving at the librarian as I went straight to the back where I'd always studied in high school.

It was quiet back there, away from everything and everyone. Other than the librarian and a few people using the computers up front, there wasn't anyone else in the building, though. School was out as of that afternoon, and I was the only person in the county trying to read my course work for the next semester. Not that I needed to, now that I'd applied to Trinity. I would have to buy all new books for my scheduled classes come fall.

But my parents didn't know that yet. No one did, and I wasn't going to say anything about it until I had everything sorted and settled. Once I had my admittance confirmed, my courses scheduled, and my books bought, no one could argue with me if they didn't like it.

Like Dad.

He couldn't wait for the fall so I would be back in Oregon, he'd said that morning after Ben left the shop. My father wanted me as far away from the sheriff as possible.

And yet there I was, waiting for the man to see my car out front and come find me.

I had no damn willpower where Ben was concerned, apparently. I knew if Dad found out about this, he would do something reckless, and I was aware I was putting Ben's life in jeopardy after the not-so-veiled threat Dad had made the night before.

Yet I couldn't stay away when Ben had asked me to meet him tonight.

Fuck.

I'd only know the guy a few days, and I was already in so far over my head, I didn't know which way was up. I was becoming a traitor to my family.

To my mom.

Maybe I needed to stay in New York a few extra days after all. Just until I was over whatever spell I'd allowed myself to fall under where Ben was concerned. It would be better for both of us, but especially for him.

Definitely safer.

"When I said meet me later, this was not what I had in mind," Ben's deep voice murmured from right behind me.

I jumped with surprise. I'd been so lost in my head, thinking about keeping him safe, I hadn't heard or even sensed him.

"Easy," he breathed at my ear, his mouth touching my neck, making me gasp and arch into the graze of his lips against my flesh. His stubble felt so damn good against my skin. Goose bumps popped up where he caressed, making me shiver deliciously, and I was grateful there were no cameras in this part of the library. "God, you taste so good, beautiful."

I lowered my lashes, savoring this stolen moment, and tears burned my eyes because I knew it was the last time I could allow this to happen. This meetup was to tell him I couldn't see him anymore—and really mean it this time.

I couldn't—wouldn't—let anything happen to Mom. And this relationship, or whatever the hell it was, would put her freedom in jeopardy. Maybe he wouldn't betray me. But Royce Campbell would be itching to get whatever dirt he could on any member of my family, and I had plenty on my mom. The thought of betraying her, even by accident, made me feel physically ill.

"B-Ben," I started, but he traced a line with his lips to my jaw, and I couldn't stop myself from turning my head and meeting his kiss.

The Earth's rotation seemed to slow down, and I kissed him back hungrily, my hands thrusting into his hair to hold on as we devoured each other with our mouths. I was stupid—this was stupid—but I just needed one more taste.

"Let's get out of here," Ben rasped when he lifted his head sometime later. "We'll go to my place."

I was on my feet before reality hit, and I stopped cold. If my dad found out about any of this, it really was going to be all over. If Mom found out, she would be so disappointed in me. And if I was honest, that bothered me more than what Dad would possibly do. Squaring my shoulders, I locked my knees and refused to give in, no matter how good his kisses were.

"I'm leaving in the morning," I told him in a voice that wasn't nearly as strong as I needed it to be, but the words alone were enough to have him jerking around to face me.

"Leaving for where?" he demanded, his jaw tense. "When will you be back?"

"I'm going to New York first thing in the morning. I…don't know when I'll be back." The longer I stayed, the better at this point, I figured. As long as I was home by the time Mom started whatever treatment her doctor wanted her to have.

"What's in New York?" he growled, jealousy coming off him in waves just as it had earlier that day when Higgins had been screwing around at the shop. The look in his eyes alone had made me worried for Higgins's life at the time, and I'd pushed him out the door to avoid bloodshed.

"I'm accompanying two of my cousins. They spend every summer with their mom's family. She can't go and asked me." Relief relaxed his face, and he reached for me again. "But I'm going to stay for a while to clear my head." He opened his mouth, probably to argue with me, but I covered it with my hand. "You haven't been listening to me, Ben. Not once. We. Can. Not. Be. Together."

Covering my hand, he pressed my palm closer to his lips, kissing it tenderly before pulling it away. "Give me one good reason why we can't, Lexa."

"Because you're the sheriff, and my family are not exactly law-abiding citizens. The DA is out for blood where they are concerned, and you work directly with him." I closed my eyes, remembering all the hurtful things Dad had said about Ben using me.

At the time, I'd started to believe it, but I just couldn't completely convince myself. Ben had no clue who I was that first night. We had too strong of a connection for whatever was going on with us to be about him using me.

But I couldn't be selfish any longer.

Mom had my complete loyalty, and Dad wasn't kidding about taking care of Ben himself. He would, and it would break what was left of my soul.

"Don't worry about Royce Campbell," Ben grumbled now. "I'm going to take care of him and prove to your father I care about you."

"Ben." I blew out a frustrated sigh. "Don't go stirring up more trouble for yourself. Campbell is a slimy bastard. Whatever you have planned is going to blow up in your face. Please," I begged, not so proud that I couldn't plead for his safety. "I'm not worth any of this. Just forget about me. I don't want to see you lose your job or something worse."

He wrapped his arms around my waist, locking me against him as his intense gaze met mine. "You are worth more than anything. Don't you ever say that to me again. You know what?

Don't ever say that again, period. I'm a grown man, baby. I can take care of myself, so stop worrying about me with Campbell and your dad. I'll take them all on if that means I can be with you."

I really liked the sound of that, but even if he could deal with Campbell, he couldn't deal with Bash Reid. No one but my mom could, and I wasn't going to drag her into the middle of this shit when she was sick.

Pushing back against his hold, I stepped away from him. Already, I felt the loss of his warmth, the scent of his cologne filling my nose, the spark that zinged through my skin and blood just from being close to him. My choice was made.

Family would always come first for me.

"Bye, Ben," I whispered, fighting the burn of tears all over again.

SEVEN

Sleep was elusive all night, and trying to get any type of rest on the plane just wasn't possible with the way Garret was constantly causing some kind of trouble.

Somehow, he stole a knife from one of the guard's leg holsters and tried to carve his name into the table at the back of the jet before any of us realized. After that, we were all wide awake, and I was ready to toss my cousin out the door without a parachute. Now I understood why Aunt Flick looked a little haggard throughout the school year, but during the summer, she was more well rested and had a little pep to her step. She needed weeks away from her son just as much as Nova needed her time in New York with her favorite person.

We were met right on the tarmac of the airport by a limo and six huge black SUVs, all of them loaded with bodyguards. I gripped Garret's wrist in my hand as we walked down the stairs, while Nova bounced down and straight into the handsome boy's arms at the bottom.

"Ryan!" she screamed as he twirled her around and around, making her giggle happily.

Standing by the car, Anya Vitucci smiled lovingly at her son and his best friend, a toddler at her feet holding her hand. The little girl was jumping up and down, talking a mile a minute, while her mother only nodded in response to whatever her daughter was chattering on about.

"You can let me go now, Lexa," Garret grumbled, but I only tightened my hold on him.

"Yeah, that's not going to happen. Your dad said if I let you out of my sight before Ciro Donati took over your care, you were likely to run off and hide in the city." Which I didn't doubt for a single second. If I had handcuffs, I would have already slapped one on his wrist and attached the other to my own for a little extra security.

Anya laughed when I got to the bottom of the stairs and Garret struggled against my hold once again. "Well, I see trouble has arrived."

He turned beet red, but shrugged. "I just wanna have fun," he complained. "Nothing wrong with that."

"No," she agreed with a smirk that made her blue eyes sparkle. "Not a single thing wrong with that, kiddo. Unless you start endangering your life or others. Now, get your smart ass in the limo before I show you what they would do to kids in Russia who 'just wanna have fun.'"

I could have fallen on my knees in gratitude for the woman with how fast Garret straightened up and did exactly as he was told with just one dark look from her. She gave me a quick, one-armed hug while her daughter danced around our feet. "Good to see you, *myshka*," she murmured before stepping back. She was so small, I felt more like a giant than normal as I stood over her. Yet at the same time, something about her made me feel tiny.

"*Myshka*," the toddler echoed, holding up her arms and grunting, wanting to be held. "*Myshka!*"

Bending, I lifted Samara into my arms. Her eyes, so like her mother's, were filled with a happiness only the purely innocent held as she hugged me trustingly. "Pweety," she said with a sigh as she snuggled into my arms and promptly fell asleep.

I was so surprised she'd fallen asleep that fast, it scared me, and I looked at Anya for guidance.

Grinning, she shook her dark head. "Don't worry. The little devil can fall asleep in the blink of an eye. First time it happened, her father thought he'd broken her and freaked out."

Having met Cristiano Vitucci on a few occasions, I found the idea of him freaking out over anything kind of ludicrous. Yet I'd seen how much he loved his wife and son; I could only imagine his precious baby daughter had him tied in knots.

Still grinning, Anya turned to her son. "Ryan, time to go. Nova is probably tired after that long flight."

"I'm not," Nova assured her as she skipped over to the older woman and embraced her. "I missed you too, Anya. Did you miss me?"

"So much. But not nearly as much as Ryan, I'm sure."

"No one misses me as much as Ryan," Nova assured her with so much confidence in her voice, I couldn't help but smile.

But the truth was, I doubted even her parents would miss her during the time she was away as much as Ryan missed her throughout the rest of the year. Whatever bond those two had, it was a strong one. Yet I worried about how painful it would be for the little cousin I'd always considered a baby sister if that bond were ever broken.

***

Even though it was my first trip to New York, everyone treated me like I was just as much a part of their family as Garret and Nova were. From Aunt Flick's cousin, Ciro, all the way to Adrian Volkov, Anya's older brother.

"You've been the talk of the morning," Theo, Adrian's son and perhaps my closest friend, confessed as we sat in some posh restaurant his family owned in the middle of the city.

I toyed with my water glass, avoiding his direct gaze. "I can only imagine."

He laughed heartily, his slightly shaggy hair falling across his forehead, his dark eyes alight with mirth. Theo was a seriously good-looking guy, but he still had a boyishness about him that reminded me of my brother, officially making it impossible for me to feel anything even remotely approaching attraction. That didn't mean the female population didn't chase after him like they were all in heat, though. Even right then, he was getting looks from the women at other tables near our own. "So, it's true, then. You're fucking around with the sheriff back in Cali."

"I'm not fucking him," I snapped. "I didn't let it get that far, and I won't. Family means everything to me... Scratch that. Fuck the rest of my family. My mom means everything to me. I would sell my soul to make sure that she's safe, that nothing touches her."

He gave me a look that had the anger in me drying up. Damn it, he knew me so well; I couldn't hide anything from him. Theo and I had bonded from the first time we met. We were both adopted by the women we loved more than life. Our moms meant everything to us, and we would do anything for them.

"Okay, okay. Take it easy. I know you don't mean that. You don't have to prove your family loyalty to me, sweetheart. You're just pissed at your dad for taking all his frustration out on you. He loves you, Lexa. You two have never been at odds before, and the only reason he's so off the walls right now is because your mom is sick. Once things have calmed down, he'll lighten up."

Guilt hit me, but I pushed it down. I'd told Theo all about Mom's cancer, knowing he would never tell a soul. When his own mom needed a kidney transplant years ago, he'd confided in me, and that was when our bond was really solidified. I'd never told anyone anything he'd confessed to me back then, and I never would. Just as I knew anything I told him, he would take to the grave.

That wasn't why I felt guilty, though. I'd told him, but I hadn't mentioned a word of Mom's illness to Ben, when I'd ached to unload it all on his shoulders. I felt like I was betraying him in some way, telling all my worries to anyone but him, which was beyond crazy.

"I'm pissed, but not so much at him as I am at myself," I admitted. "I knew I was being reckless when this whole thing started with Ben. People from my world don't date people from his."

"You make it sound like you are some poor white trash from the wrong side of the tracks. Your parents are loaded, girl."

That had me rolling my eyes. "No, they're comfortable, but they aren't millionaires or anything. Not like your family, Theo. We all still have to work for our paychecks."

"As does the sheriff, I'm assuming," Theo pointed out. "Stop putting yourself down."

"I wasn't," I lied.

"Bullshit."

"Ugh, you're so annoying. Why are we friends again?" But a ghost of a smile teased at my lips, and he winked at me as he picked up a fork and knife, cutting into the steak the waiter had just placed in front of him.

Once the waiter was gone and I sat there glaring at the salmon on my own plate, Theo cleared his throat. "I should warn you. Everyone is determined to set the two of us up."

"I figured as much. Aunt Flick and Mom were both hinting at it last night, encouraging me to stay a few extra days." I'd packed enough clothes to stay for at least a week, hoping that was enough time to clear my head before I went home to help Mom once she started her cancer treatments.

"And you're okay with that?" He sounded skeptical enough for me to lift my gaze from my food to find him frowning.

"You and I both know we are only ever going to be friends. Let them have their fantasies about us becoming a couple and then getting married and having all those grandbabies my dad says he never wants but secretly craves."

His lips twitched with humor once again. "I'd marry you in a heartbeat if my emotions weren't already involved elsewhere."

I snorted out a laugh. "I don't think it would work out, Theo. I'm just not your type. This friendship would go down the drain if we had to spend more than a few days together every few years. We're better as long-distance besties who text so we can bitch about our lives to each other."

"I agree." Leaning forward, he got a sly look in his dark eyes that had my own narrowing on him. "But the parents don't need to know that, do they?"

Picking up my knife, I pointed it at him. "Stop it right there, Volkov. Don't think one more thing, or you'll find yourself without a tongue. I won't play those kinds of mind games with my mom."

Roaring with laughter, he grabbed the knife from my hand before I could even blink and turned it so it was now pointing in my direction. "Okay, okay. We won't pretend to date to appease my own mother. I just thought maybe if your sheriff thought you were otherwise engaged, he would back off."

I opened my mouth to tell him no again, but I quickly closed it. I didn't like lying to anyone, especially my mom, but it wasn't the worst idea to have as a backup plan if I got home and Ben didn't keep his distance.

"I'll think about it," I told him after a moment.

"It's an open invitation," he vowed. "Anytime you need me to step in and help out, I'll be the dashing fiancé who rides to the rescue."

"Noted," I muttered and finally took a bite of my dinner. As I chewed, I stewed it over before releasing a heavy sigh. "Theo?"

"Yeah, sweets?"

"Thanks."

That earned me another wink. "Anytime."

EIGHT

BEN

I drummed my fingers impatiently on the steering wheel as I waited for the others to arrive, glaring out into the darkness because I just wanted this shit over with.

Beside me, Mayor Jenkins sipped his coffee calmly, trying to ignore my chaotic energy when we both knew he was just as anxious for this to end and to get away from me in the mood I was currently in.

Lexa had been gone for over a week. On top of my not being able to see her, she still hadn't unblocked me, and every text I sent was kicked back. It was driving me crazy—this need to see her, to touch her. To just fucking be near her.

Things were already in motion to get Campbell taken care of, but I needed the MC to be on board with it too. I had no choice but to ask Jenkins to use his connection with the club to set up this secret meeting. Which brought us to now, the two of us sitting in my personal truck waiting on Bash Reid and whoever else he happened to bring along to have this chat with me.

Finally, I heard the roar of motorcycles in the distance and wrapped my fingers around the steering wheel. My first reaction as I saw the four motorcycles pull into the old trailer park off the beaten path was to jump out of the truck and knock Bash the fuck out. I knew he was the reason Lexa was in New York and not there with me. He was why we weren't together, and I wanted to tear him apart limb by limb.

But that would only push Lexa away more; that much I knew. So, I squeezed the wheel until my fingers went numb as the bikers turned off their engines and casually climbed off them.

Jenkins opened the passenger door and got out, greeting the four men like they were family, while I took my time opening my own door and stepping out.

As I slowly walked toward them, I noticed the other three with Bash. Masterson was on his left, with Hawk and Jet Hannigan on his right. I was taller than the two Hannigans, but just as wide as Masterson and Lexa's father, so their size didn't even begin to intimidate me as I reached them and met their glares one at a time.

"What's this about, Jenks?" Bash asked the mayor as he crossed his arms over his cut.

"Ben needed your ear," the old man informed him. "And I think you're going to want to hear everything the boy has to say."

"Doubtful," Masterson said with a snort.

Hawk stepped forward. "Let's give the kid the chance to speak."

I wasn't surprised he was the most reasonable of the group. His wife was a killer defense attorney, but outside of court, she was one of the sweetest women I'd ever met. I didn't mind so much getting raked over the coal fires of hell by her on the witness stand because I knew how much time she put into volunteering at the local women's shelter just outside of town. Hawk acted as the shelter's muscle part time, and I'd been called out to help with a couple disturbances in the past few months.

"I've got a connection at the attorney general's office. I called in a favor, and Royce Campbell is being investigated. Starting tomorrow, every election he's ever campaigned in to become DA will be scrutinized…along with other things."

My announcement seemed to stun all four men because they dropped their menacingly crossed arms and just stood there blinking at me.

"Hold up," Jet said after a few seconds of dazed silence. "First of all, you realize this will stir up all kinds of shit for you at work, right? Campbell is a vindictive motherfucker. He's going to make your life miserable if he ever finds out you're putting his position at risk."

I shrugged. "If he finds out, he finds out. I'm not worried about it. But this investigation is secret. Other than the investigator, the only people who know about this are the six of us."

"Okay. Second… Why the fuck would you do this? We all thought you were working with that little bitch to get dirt on us. You were using Lexa…"

"Shut your fucking mouth!" I roared, taking a step closer to him, making everyone tense. "I would never use her. I don't give two goddamn fucks about what you and your club do as long as you're not stirring up shit around here. You keep spreading that shit and filling her head with it, and I'll cave your head in."

Jenkins put a hand on my arm, trying to tug me back, and I breathed deeply through my nose, trying to clear the red haze that was blinding me.

Jet surprised me by laughing, not in the least bit worried about what I could—and would—do to him if he kept running his mouth. "Point made, Sheriff." He nudged Bash with his elbow. "Looks like this boy is all right."

Other than a grunt, Bash was quiet for a long moment, his eyes so much like Lexa's drilling through me to see beneath to my soul. "Do you really care about my daughter, Davis?" he finally demanded.

"Sir," I told him, looking him straight in the eye. "I think I love her."

"Love?" he muttered, skeptical. "You've known her for all of, what? Two weeks? And half that time, she's been in another state."

Masterson cleared his throat beside him. "Don't knock it, man. Just because you eased into loving Raven doesn't mean love can't come that quick. You know how it was for Willa and me."

"But she's just a baby," Bash growled. "Barely nineteen. And he's what? Fucking thirty?"

"Age is only a number," Jet told him with a shrug. "Besides, at least he's not trying to sneak around behind your back. He's man enough to tell you to your face he's in love with the girl."

The MC president's face tightened, and I suspected that his brother-in-law was throwing some serious shade at him. Muttering vicious curses under his breath, Bash turned on his heel and walked back to his motorcycle. Bellowing those same curses up at the sky, he threw his adult tantrum while I stood there with the other men.

"Should we be aware of who the special investigator is?" Hawk asked, ignoring his brother-in-law.

"I don't even know who it is," I told him honestly. "It's better for everyone if no one is aware of who they are, so they aren't getting added attention drawn in their direction."

"Understandable," he said with a nod. "Whatever you find out, though, we would appreciate it if you kept us informed. And if you need anything, just say the word. Someone will make it happen."

"And him?" I lifted my chin in Bash's direction. "Do I need to watch my back with that one?"

"You want to fuck his daughter. What do you think?" Smirking, Hawk thrust his hand forward. "Don't worry about the father-in-law. He will come around. We did after he snuck around with our baby sister for fuck knows how long. This is just karma coming back to bite him in the ass."

As I shook Hawk's hand, I tightened my grip around it and asked the one question I'd been aching to know all week. "How is Lexa?"

His brows pinched together. "You haven't spoken to her?"

Releasing his hand, I stepped back with a shrug. "She blocked me. I haven't spoken to her since before she left."

"She's good," Jet answered for him. "She will be coming home next Sunday."

"That's more than another week away." I swallowed my groan, wondering what the fuck I was going to do until then. I needed to hear her voice, damn it.

"Son, a week ain't nothing. You'll survive." Nodding his head at me, Jet walked over to his bike.

The other two followed, but I stood there, waiting, knowing this wasn't over.

Seconds later, Bash proved me right as he stomped back to me and poked me in the chest with his index finger. "I won't stand in your way anymore, but it's her choice. If she wants you, she can fucking have you. But if she doesn't, you respect that and leave her alone."

"Yes, sir."

"And you come to me if shit gets too tight with Campbell. You might not care what happens to you, but people in this town already know about you and Lexa. That puts a target on her back if Campbell wants to go after you."

Fuck, I hadn't even thought of that, but I should have.

"If he even looks at her wrong, he's a dead man," I vowed, my voice laced with all the rage that wanted to be given free rein.

Bash relaxed slightly, his blue eyes assessing me thoughtfully before he dropped his hand and stepped back. "You break her heart, I'll break your neck," he warned before walking away.

As the four bikers rode away, Jenkins slapped me on the back, a smile on his wrinkled face. "You won that war, boy. Now what are you going to do?"

"Wait for my woman to get back so I can tell her she's mine."

NINE

"Are you sure you feel up to taking all of this on, honey?" Mom said as she handed over the keys to all the companies she took care of.

For as long as I could remember, Mom had kept the books for all the MC businesses. From Uncle Spider's tattoo shop to the construction company owned by my dad's cousin Tanner and his wife, Jos. That included the Hannigans' bar as well as Dad and Trigger's garage.

"Mom, I'll be fine," I assured her as I bent and hugged her.

From the moment she'd gotten home from the hospital that morning, she'd been trying to do everything all at once. It had taken Dad carrying her to bed—and Uncle Jet and him standing over her threateningly to keep her there—to get her to take things easy like her doctor had said after her full hysterectomy the day before.

Since she'd agreed to her doctor taking everything, we'd been told that the risk of her cancer cells spreading was low, but she would still have to undergo chemotherapy treatments. Dad and I had been relieved it was only three sessions, until Dr. Weller said they were the strongest treatments possible.

Which meant Mom was most likely going to be so sick, she wouldn't be able to work for a while. After talking it over the night before, I told Dad I wanted to take over more of Mom's responsibilities. Which included the accounting books for the other MC-run businesses—at least, the legit businesses. I knew there was no way any of them was going to let me look at the books that weren't supposed to exist.

"I know you will, but this is a lot for you to have to take on, Lexa. You should be enjoying your summer off before you have to head back to school." Her voice turned sad, and her green eyes filled with tears.

Those tears felt like acid being poured right onto my heart. "Mom…I was going to wait until I had everything finalized, but I dropped out of Oregon and enrolled in Trinity. I got my acceptance letter in my email last week."

If I thought my announcement would dry up her tears, I was wrong. "Really?" she sobbed. "You're going to stay?"

"You're not happy?" I asked, feeling tears start to fill my own eyes.

"I'm th-thrilled," she cried, putting her face in her hands. "I miss you so much when you're that far away."

"Mom…" I hugged her again, but I glanced at Dad for help over her shoulder.

His face was tight, his hands balled into fists at his sides, and he couldn't hide the tears in his eyes. This was killing him just as much as it was me. Mom was so strong, and now her emotions were all over the place, completely out of her control. Dr. Weller had told us this was likely to happen, but I hadn't really given it much thought. Mom didn't cry at the drop of a hat. Hell, until recently, I'd rarely ever seen her shed a tear.

Beneath me, she felt small and fragile, and I eased the pressure of my hug, afraid I might hurt her if I wasn't more careful. But before I could straighten, she wrapped her arms around me, showing me she still had that same strength I'd always relied on. "Thank you, baby. It means so much to me that you're going to be home from now on."

A light tap on the door was followed by Aunt Flick coming in with a tray of soup and sandwiches. Walking over, she ignored Mom's tears as she placed the tray across her lap and then opened the bottle of pain pills on the bedside table.

"I don't want those," Mom complained, wiping her eyes as she glared at the little brown bottle. "They make me loopy, and all I do is sleep."

"Good," Dad growled, half under his breath. When she shot him a hard look, he shrugged. "You have to stay ahead of the pain. You might not feel any now, but you will soon. Please don't torture me by having to watch you go through that."

Her beautiful face softened, and she held out her hand for the pill Aunt Flick offered. Popping it into her mouth, she swallowed it with a drink of the juice on her tray. "Happy?"

"For now."

While they were distracted, I quickly made my getaway. Walking down the hall to my bedroom, I grimaced when I saw my case full of dirty clothes along with all the new ones I'd bought while in New York. None of them had been purchased by me. Between Anya Volkov and Theo's mom, Victoria, I hadn't had to spend a single penny of my own money, even though I'd protested that they didn't need to buy me anything.

The two women hadn't taken no for an answer, though, and I knew it was because they thought I was going to be a part of their family soon if they had their way.

Unfortunately for them, this was one thing they wouldn't be getting their way on. Theo and I were just friends, and that was the way it was going to stay. Not only because I still hadn't figured out how to turn off what I felt for Ben in the more than two weeks I'd been away from him. But because Theo had his own relationship issues that I wasn't about to explain to either his aunt or his mother.

Placing my keys by my phone, I started sorting through my case. I hadn't unpacked when

I got home Sunday evening, too anxious about Mom's surgery scheduled for Monday morning. Then we were at the hospital all day, and I hadn't gotten back to the house until late last night. I wouldn't have left when I did, but Dad and the rest of the family had insisted, and I'd driven Max to Tanner and Jos's before coming home and crashing.

There weren't just new clothes to be dealt with, but some new makeup and even a few pieces of jewelry. The makeup, I was sort of happy about. After Victoria taught me how to contour to minimize the appearance of my scar, I'd actually started pushing my hair back from my face. I'd never been one to wear a lot of makeup, but after a few lessons, I seriously didn't recognize myself without the scar being so glaringly obvious now.

Once the dirty clothes were in my hamper, I hung up all the new ones and then grabbed the keys and my purse before heading out. Mom had given me her schedule of when she did each business's books, and today was Aggie's normal time.

The parking lot was crowded when I pulled in and tried to find a place to park. The only spot was at the back of the lot near the dumpster. Gagging at the stench coming from all that trash basically cooking in the sun, I hurried into the diner.

As soon as I opened the door, Aunt Quinn was there, asking me how Mom was feeling.

"She's emotional today. And stubbornly not wanting to take her pain meds, but Dad is watching her like a hawk." I held up the keys to the file cabinet where Mom kept the diner's account books. "Hope you don't mind. I'm going to be taking on some of Mom's jobs until she's back on her feet."

"No, no. Of course not. You go on back to the office, and I'll bring you something to eat." She was practically pushing me toward the back now, and I laughed at how strong she was for such a small woman.

"I'm not all that hungry," I tried to assure her, but she wasn't going to take no for an answer. "Okay, okay. But could I use the bathroom first?"

Sighing heavily, she paused and nodded. "Yeah. You might as well. You're going to see it eventually anyway."

"See what?" I mused, brows lifted at her.

"He's in the back," Aunt Quinn said, as if I should know who "he" was. "And he's not alone. He hasn't been alone for over a week now."

"He?" I muttered, but something clenched in my gut, and I knew exactly who she was talking about—even if I wanted to pretend I didn't.

"Just put on a smile and don't let him hurt you," my aunt commanded as I walked around her.

As I rounded the corner that would take me to the bathroom, I spotted him right in the back. He sat facing the rest of the hungry lunch crowd, but his full attention was on the person sitting in front of him. At my first sight of him in over two weeks, I felt my stomach tighten, and I ached to go over and sit beside him. To tell him how much I'd missed him.

To just be near him.

He had more than a few days of scruff on his jaw, and I wondered if he was growing out a beard. I liked it on him. A lot. And I couldn't help imagining how his facial hair would feel against my cheek when he kissed me. But the dark circles under his eyes distracted me from that train of thought, and I couldn't help thinking he'd been getting about as much sleep as I had during the time I'd been gone.

Then the person he was with shifted, and all I saw was a cloud of lustrous blond hair. My concern for Ben died a sudden and painful death as I watched her put her hand on the one of his that was wrapped around his mug of coffee, just as I heard a husky, flirty laugh come from her. And he didn't pull away. My gaze zeroed in on her touching him, and what Aunt Quinn said earlier finally made sense.

"He's not alone. He hasn't been alone for over a week now."

Did that mean he was with the blonde now? As in *with her*, with her?

Whatever the blonde was saying had Ben's lips lifting in a half smile, and I felt like someone had punched me dead center in the chest.

When I left for New York, I'd gone to clear my head and put what I was feeling for Ben into perspective. I hadn't really thought about what he would be up to while I was gone. He seemed so into me, the thought of him moving on while I was away just didn't enter my head.

But it should have.

Because obviously, he had.

Suddenly, I couldn't quite catch my breath. He'd moved on so easily, while I'd been losing my mind just trying to stop thinking about him twenty-four seven. The guilt I felt only mounted each day because I couldn't stop what I was feeling, and I felt like I was letting everyone in my family down because of it.

Meanwhile, he was back here in Creswell Springs getting on with his life, while I was stuck in some damn limbo.

If I was so forgettable, maybe he'd been trying to use me after all.

Realizing that made me feel sick, and I turned away from the sight of the guy I realized I wasn't going to stop caring about just because I had to. Walking back toward the office, I passed Aunt Quinn.

"Lexa—"

"I have work to do," I said in a tone devoid of all emotion. "And I'm not hungry, so please don't waste food I'm not going to eat."

"Honey, I'm sorry," she tried to soothe, but I knew if she hugged me, I would cry.

TEN

Paige brushed her hand over mine, finally releasing me after Campbell got up from his table three booths to my right.

"Why do I feel dirty whenever that creep is around?" she hissed as she sat back, picking up her cup of coffee and taking a leisurely sip.

I grunted, but as she sat back, clearing my field of vision, a flash of dark hair caught my attention and the air suddenly seemed to be trapped in my chest.

Lexa.

And she was walking away.

"Ben!" Paige called after me, but I was already chasing after Lexa. "Where the hell are you going?"

"Go back to my office. I'll be there when I finish here," I tossed over my shoulder.

"Sheriff," Quinn greeted as I caught sight of Lexa's hair again, this time going into the back of the diner where the office was. "I wouldn't recommend it."

I didn't even spare her a glance as I jogged down the little hall and pushed open the office door just as it started to swing closed in my face.

The first thing I noticed was how tense her shoulders were, and I wrapped my arms around her from behind, pulling her back hard against my front as I buried my face in her neck. She stiffened in my arms as I inhaled her scent like it was the first breath of air I'd had in weeks.

"No!" she cried and savagely jerked out of my arms to face me. "Don't touch me."

Ignoring the fire in her eyes telling me to keep my distance, I cupped her face in both hands. She had on makeup, but I wasn't sure I liked it because it was hiding her natural beauty.

"I missed you so much, Lexa," I growled, brushing my lips over hers.

Laughing dryly, she pushed against my chest, but she was unable to budge me. Her head jerked back, and she glared up at me. "Yeah, it was obvious you missed me. How long did you wait, Ben? Did you find someone else the second I left, or did you wait a few days before moving on to the next conquest?"

There was fury blazing in her glacier-blue eyes, but she couldn't keep the hurt from lacing her voice. "You think I moved on?" I demanded. Grabbing hold of her waist, I locked her against me, making her feel just how much agony my body was in after weeks away from her. "How could I possibly move on when you are all I see?"

"Smooth line, Sheriff," she seethed. "But I'm not buying it. I see straight through your bullshit now. Tell me something? Was it just a game to you? Did you like chasing after the MC princess and making her bow to your every whim so easily?"

If she were anyone else yelling at me like that, I would have walked away without a backward glance. But she wasn't just anyone. "God, you're maddening. You know that, right? Give me two minutes to explain certain things to you, and you can calm down."

"Calm down?" she repeated before pushing at my chest. "I am perfectly calm, asshole."

Frustrated, I released her. Walking away a few steps, I shut the door and flipped the lock just in case someone tried to interrupt us. "You saw me having lunch with Paige, is that it? You're jealous I was eating with her?"

"Is that what you were doing?" She *hmphed.* "Looked a little more intimate than that."

At least she wasn't denying she was jealous, I mused to myself. "It wasn't anything more than two friends having a meal together, Lexa."

"Whatever. I'm not going to argue about this with you. I have work to do, and I'm sure you do too, Sheriff." After walking around the desk, she sat and turned on the computer. "I won't keep you from doing your job or your…friend."

"Did you have meals with any friends while you were in New York?" I demanded, trying to get her to see reason.

Her gaze lifted from the screen in front of her, her eyes narrowed on me. "Plenty of times, actually. But I'd never fucked my friend. Can you say the same?"

Fuck. I didn't know how to answer that. I'd dated Paige. We'd had a pretty hot sex life during our relationship, but once I realized she was trying to change me, any attraction I'd had for her had turned to ash.

"See?" she said, her eyes still flashing flames as high as the gates of hell. Leaning back, she crossed her arms over her chest, lifting her brows. "So, this 'friend'? Does that include benefits? Or was she someone special?"

Scrubbing my hands over my face, I leaned back against the door, wondering how the hell we'd gotten from me only wanting to hold her, to her wanting to talk about my ex. "She's an old girlfriend, baby. We dated for like six months, and then I broke up with her when she tried to turn me into something I'll never be."

"What was that, exactly?"

"She wanted me to turn my military background into a political career, like her father."

Lexa snorted, shaking her head. "And yet, here you are. Turning your military background into a political career by running for sheriff in the fall."

"The irony isn't lost on me," I assured her, unable to keep my eyes from devouring the sight of her sitting only feet away from me. "But my career choices weren't the only thing she wanted to change about me. My ink was too much for her. She wanted me to get anything that was easily visible removed. In her eyes, my size was too bulky, and she wanted me to get leaner. I'm not good enough for her like this, Lexa. Maybe if I'd loved her, I could have changed and been okay with it. But there was never that tight of a connection with us."

She looked away, frowning at the computer screen. "Well, it looks like she's over wanting to change you. The way she was touching you earlier screamed she likes you enough to take you as you are."

"That isn't what's going on with us," I told her as I pushed away from the door and stalked toward her. "Come to my apartment tonight, and I'll explain everything."

"No way," she snapped. "I don't care enough to know what is going on with you and your bitchy ex. Thanks, but no thanks."

Putting one hand on the back of her chair and the other on the desk in front of her, I leaned down so that our noses were nearly touching. "Lexa, I haven't seen you in two and a half weeks. Come to my apartment. Let me explain about Paige and everything else that has been going on while you were away. I doubt your father told you, but I talked to him and—"

"Wait!" she cut me off, leaning her head back and putting inches between us. "You spoke to my dad? And you're still breathing?"

I grinned and pushed closer, touching my lips to the corner of her mouth. "Believe it, beautiful."

"Fine," she breathed. "I...I'll think about stopping by."

Cupping the back of her head, I kissed her quickly. "I get off work at eight." Straightening, I pulled my keys out of my pocket and took off the extra I'd had made to my apartment weeks before just for her. "If you get there before me, use this and make yourself comfortable."

Hesitantly, she took the key from me and dropped it onto the desk beside the keyboard. "If I can make it, I will. But I'm not going to promise anything. My mom might need me."

That had me pausing. "I've heard a few things about her the last two days. Is it true? Is she battling cancer?"

Lexa lowered her lashes, swallowing hard, but she nodded. "Cervical cancer. She had surgery yesterday. Dr. Weller told us before surgery that the labs showed her cancer was already pretty far advanced, but hopefully, the hysterectomy got it all. She still has to have a few chemo treatments, though."

"Baby, I'm so sorry. If there is anything your parents need, just tell me."

Her smile was sad when she met my gaze. "Thanks, but they have it all covered for now. I think I'm more scared for her to endure the chemo than I was the surgery."

Crouching down, I took both her hands in mine. "Whatever happens, I'm here for you. Just remember that, Lexa."

"Th-thanks," she whispered just as a hard knock came on the door.

"Lexa?" Quinn called out. "Do I need to call your dad, honey?"

Sighing, she pushed the chair back and stood. "You should go. I'm busy, and I honestly don't know how long this is going to take."

Straightening, I grasped her hand and brought her palm to my lips, kissing the center. "I'll see you tonight?"

"If I can," she promised with a nod.

"Lexa!" Quinn shouted. "I'm about to call Bash if you don't come out of there right now."

Groaning, she hurried over to the door and opened it. "It's fine, Aunt Quinn. Sheriff Davis was just leaving. Weren't you, Ben?"

Stopping behind her, I kissed the back of Lexa's head before turning my focus on Quinn. "Excuse me, ladies." Moving past them both, I turned once I was on the other side of the door, and I looked at Lexa over the top of her aunt's head. Lifting my hand to my ear, I motioned for her to call me and got a single nod before I forced myself to walk away.

ELEVEN

The sound of the television on in the living room pulled me toward it when I got home from Aggie's. To my surprise, Max and Dad were both sitting on the couch, plates of spaghetti in hand as they watched a baseball game.

"How's Mom feeling?" I asked as I dropped down between them.

"She's sleeping. Flick is napping beside her in case she needs help getting up to go to the bathroom." Dad offered me a piece of his garlic roll, but I only shook my head. Aunt Quinn had put one plate after another in front of me all afternoon, and I was so stuffed, I could barely breathe.

The three of us sat there in silence for a while before my curiosity got the better of me. "I didn't even think you lived here anymore," I teased my brother with a grin. "Figured Tanner and Jos adopted you and you were their son."

He grumbled something under his breath before placing his now-empty plate on the coffee table. "Figured I needed to stay home more often. No one tells you shit when you're not around."

"Your mom didn't want you to worry, boy," Dad told him in a hard voice.

"Yeah, well, I'm worried now," Max bit out, used to our father growling at him. "You should have told me she was sick when you first found out. I bet Lexa knew from day one, and she's not even her real mom!"

Pain sliced through me like shrapnel, and I couldn't hold in my gasp at being attacked so brutally. No one, and I mean no one, had ever tossed that in my face before. Raven was my mom in every sense of the word except for biologically. But she never let that stop her from loving me, and I'd never gotten hung up on the fact that I was the oddball of the family because I didn't share a single drop of Hannigan blood.

Having my brother, whom I'd always been close with growing up, say such a thing now stung.

I jumped to my feet, glaring from one Reid male to the next. "You know what? I'm getting sick and tired of you two acting like total douchebags and throwing shit in my face. If it weren't for Mom, I'd say to hell with you all and never come back to this house."

"Lexa," Max started, his face contrite. "I'm sorry. I didn't mean it. I…I'm just pissed."

"That doesn't give you the right to take it out on me," I snapped at him, and he flinched. "Between the two of you, you make me feel like I don't even belong to this family anymore." My glare went to Dad. "Yes, I know everyone is tense because of Mom's cancer. I'm scared and worried too. But tearing me down to make yourselves feel better is not the way to deal with it. And I'm tired of having to tiptoe around everyone else's feelings just to avoid getting lashed out at."

"Lexa." Dad reached for my hand, but I backed away. "Sweetheart, I'm sorry. I never should have talked to you like that a few weeks ago. I regretted it as soon as it happened, but I was only trying to protect your mom."

"I get that," I said with a nod. "But you really could have handled that a little differently without making me seem like a traitor to this family."

"So, you really were screwing around with the sheriff?" Max butted in.

"No!" I seethed. "I didn't screw around with the sheriff. We were flirting and—"

"I really don't need to know the details, sis," he muttered, lifting his hands in surrender. "And you don't have to explain yourself to me. I don't even know the guy, so I'll trust your judgment on him. I was just wondering about the rumors is all."

Dad stood, but instead of snarling at either of us, he pulled me for a tight hug. "Lexa, if Davis is who you want, I'm not going to stand in your way anymore. The two of us had a...chat. And I told him if you choose him, then I'd respect that. But if you didn't, he needed to respect your decision and leave you alone."

Stunned, I just stood there, letting Dad hold me. What Ben said was true, then. He'd spoken to Dad. And survived. Maybe I should go to his place later and give him a chance to explain about that Paige woman after all.

"And I really am sorry for the way I talked to you. I couldn't wrap my head around Raven's cancer, then there you were with a guy for the first time. I lost my mind, and I reacted badly. I hate that I hurt you."

Something I'd noticed about my dad over the years was that he rarely apologized. Unless it was to Mom. He was Bash Reid, Angel's Halo Motorcycle Club president. He didn't need to say sorry, ever.

Yet there he was, apologizing to me.

It didn't make the sting of Max's throwaway comment about Mom not being my real mom hurt any less, but it went a long way toward healing what Dad had scraped raw weeks before.

"Do you mean it?" I asked hesitantly as I looked up into those eyes that were identical to my own. "Do you really not care if I'm with Ben?"

He sighed heavily but nodded. "I don't care, Lexa. After our talk, I realized Davis would be a better ally than an enemy."

As apology presents went, that was the best one he ever could have given me.

Standing on my tiptoes, I kissed his cheek. "Thanks, Dad."

Max jumped to his feet. Even at fifteen, he was almost as tall as our father, just a leaner version of him. "Does this mean you forgive me too?"

The smile that had started to form on my lips died, and I glared at him standing there with his arms open wide to embrace me. "You're still on my shit list," I told him as I walked toward the stairs. "And don't you ever say that again, asshole!"

"Lex, I really am sorry," he whined as I stomped upstairs. "Come back. Love me!"

"Dude, you gotta get smoother. If that's how you are with the chicks, your game is lacking." I heard Dad admonishing him.

"Gross, Dad. I'm not talking about the action I get with you."

Snickering to myself, I went to my room to shower and change. There was still plenty of time before Ben got off work, and I wanted to look my best when I showed up at his place.

But excitement was making my blood zing, and I couldn't wait to see him again. I couldn't remember ever feeling so…freaking giddy. As I washed my hair, I even found myself humming a little, a smile glued to my lips as I laughed at myself for being so off-key.

When I was finished, I dried my hair and put on a little makeup. I didn't contour like I'd done earlier in the day because I'd noticed Ben hadn't seemed to like it. I didn't know why, but the way his eyes had skimmed over my face told me he wasn't a fan of that look on me. That made me wonder if he'd stopped seeing the scar, if he just didn't care about it now.

I could hope.

Once I was ready, I walked down to Mom's room and knocked lightly before sticking my head in to check on her. She was sitting up in bed, a new tray across her lap, this time with spaghetti and garlic rolls.

"Lexa," she greeted me with a tired smile as I entered her bedroom. Seeing I was dressed to go out, her eyes lit up. "You look beautiful, baby."

Crossing to her bed, I climbed in beside her, snuggling against her like I used to when I was a little girl. "How are you feeling?" I asked as I tucked the covers over both our legs.

"Those damn pain pills make me so tired. Flick just made me take another one after she brought my dinner. Between her and your dad, I'm feeling a little overwhelmed, honey." She blew out a frustrated sigh and leaned her head against my shoulder. "You're the only sane one right now, kiddo."

Kissing the top of her head, I closed my eyes, thankful she was there with me. "I don't know how sane I am, Mom. I...I need to tell you something."

Her head snapped up, her eyes going from tired to assessing in an instant. Before my eyes, she went into mom mode, and I wanted to cry then and there because I never wanted to lose her. "You know you can tell me anything. No matter how bad, I won't judge you, and I'll do whatever I can to help. Even if it means having to get rid of a body."

"I know," I whispered before clearing my throat. I didn't want to cry in front of her, not when everyone else was driving her bonkers. "I love you, Mom. More than any person in the world. Please know that."

"I do, Lexa." She caught my hand, entwining our fingers. "And I love you just as much."

"I like Ben Davis," I confessed. "As in, I could maybe fall in love with him."

"Sheriff Davis?"

I nodded, my teeth sinking into my bottom lip as I waited for her reaction.

Her smile shouldn't have surprised me, but it did. "You like him that much?" I nodded. "You know, I always worried you would be too picky. That you wouldn't let a guy close enough to give him your heart. I'm not an easy person to love, and I know I've kind of infused that into you over the years. But I prayed you would find someone who would be good enough for you. Someone who would fight for you."

"You're not a hard person to love," I tried to reassure her, but she only rolled her eyes.

"Please, Lexa. To you, I'm Wonder Woman, but to the rest of the world, I'm a hard-ass. And I like it that way. You're the only person who matters when it comes to seeing me as a superhero. I always liked being your mentor, the one person you looked up to the most."

"Wonder Woman is a kick-ass role model," I told her.

Laughing softly, she kissed my cheek. "We're getting off topic here, kid. What I'm saying is that Ben seems to be the kind of guy I always wanted for you. Dad told me about their little meeting. The sheriff had a set of balls on him to risk meeting your dad like he did. He's putting himself at risk for this plan of his, but I think he knows what he's doing. I hope, at least."

"What plan?" I demanded, sitting up straighter. "How will he be putting himself at risk?"

She grimaced. "I should let him tell you. That's where you're heading to now, isn't it?" The grimace turned into a smirk, and I gave a nonchalant shrug. "Let him explain since this is his idea."

"But you're okay with me dating Ben?" I watched her closely for any sign that she didn't like the idea of me being with a lawman, but I couldn't see any.

"If he's who you really want, I would never stand in your way, Lexa. I only ever want your happiness, and if he makes you happy, then go for it, baby girl." She pulled my head down to her chest, kissing the top of my head as she hugged me against her. "And if your dad gives you a hard time about it, just let me know. I'll set his ass straight."

Laughing, I lifted my head. "I really do love you more than anyone else, Mom. Always."

"Back at you, sweetheart. Forever."

TWELVE

I sat with Mom for over an hour, catching her up on everything that happened on my trip to New York, while she told me any juicy gossip I might have missed while I was gone. I was so wrapped up in spending time with her, I didn't realize what time it was.

By the time I got to Ben's apartment, it was twenty after eight. Jumping out of my car, I walked up the two flights of stairs to his second-story apartment in the old brick house someone had converted into four apartments. It was a nice place, one I'd always admired whenever I passed it.

Ben gave me a key, but I didn't know if I should use it or just knock. I knew he was home because I'd parked beside his work SUV. Groaning at my own indecision, I lifted my hand to knock, only to notice the door wasn't shut completely.

Frowning, I pushed it open a little and started to walk in. But before I could call out to announce I was there, I stumbled back when I caught sight of Ben.

There was a straight view from the living room back into the kitchen. He was leaning against the counter, but he didn't see me.

How could he when he had Paige wrapped around him, kissing him. Her long blond hair curled down her back, his fingers tangling in the locks as they bit into her sides. I could feel the tension in the air from where I was standing on trembling legs.

All the oxygen left my lungs in a rush, and I suddenly felt violently ill.

He'd kissed me like that the first night I met him. Savagely, like he couldn't get enough of my taste. And now he was tearing my heart from my chest.

Turning away from the sight of his hands—his fucking mouth—on someone else, I stumbled down the steps and ran back to my car.

It wasn't until I was behind the wheel, blindly trying to start the damn vehicle that I realized I was crying.

Sonofabitch.

How could I have been so blind not to see he was playing games with me? He knew I would give in and come to his place when he asked me to. And he knew I would find him with Paige.

No doubt, he was laughing his head off about how stupid and gullible I was. The fucking sad part was, he was right.

Time after time, I'd given in and succumbed to everything he'd wanted. There was no reason to think I wouldn't have this time too.

I was just a toy, a damn plaything for him to pass the time with. And even though he was with someone else now, he still wanted to continue the game. See how far he could push me, make me fall for him.

Fisting my hands around the leather of the steering wheel, I breathed in deeply, and with my next exhale, I turned my heart to ice.

To hell with Ben Davis.

I started to put the car in gear to get the hell out of there, but something stopped me.

Was I really just going to walk away after he'd set this up to hurt me? Who the fuck did he think he was?

The truth was, I didn't know who he was now.

But I sure as hell knew who I was. I was Raven Hannigan Reid's daughter, and I wasn't going to run away without letting that sonofabitch know he couldn't play games with me and walk away unscathed.

Hitting the button for my trunk, I calmly stepped out and walked around to the back of the car. There lay two possible weapons. A tire iron and a baseball bat. The bat, Mom had put there when she and Dad had handed over the keys to the car when I graduated from high school. For protection, she'd said.

Grinning, I picked it up and walked over to Ben's work SUV. The streetlights were on and showcased the vehicle perfectly as I swung the bat and broke both taillights. I didn't try to kid myself that I was strong enough to take out the back window, but I sure as fuck tried. The first sound of cracking glass was music to my sobbing heart.

Once I was satisfied with the cracks in the back glass, I moved around to the front, breaking out the headlights before smashing both side mirrors.

I was so caught up in what I was doing, I didn't even notice the cop car pull up behind me. Or the deputy who jumped out of his car with his gun drawn.

"Put the bat down, and step away from the vehicle," a deep voice boomed behind me.

Pissed at being interrupted, I turned toward the guy. I vaguely recognized the man. I thought his name was Murphy, but I wasn't sure. It wasn't like I kept up with the names of all the cops in this town.

"Put the bat down!" he repeated, his voice shaking.

I nearly laughed. This was probably the most exciting thing he'd experienced in this damn little town. There wasn't a lot of crime, and other than when Enzo Fontana tried to take out my father's MC a few times, there hadn't been much to talk about.

Thinking of Fontana had the laughter dying before it could be released, and I lifted the bat over my head and brought it down onto the hood of the SUV with all my strength, putting a nice dent across the middle. Drawing back, I did the same thing to the driver's door.

No sooner had the bat made contact than was I tackled by Murphy.

He wrestled me to the ground, throwing the bat away from us so I wasn't able to use it on him if I decided to. I struggled, but he outweighed me. My face was pushed into the asphalt, and I cursed him viciously as he squeezed my arm while putting the cuffs on me.

By the time he stood and lifted me to my feet, we were both out of breath.

"You're under arrest for destruction of county property," he wheezed out as he put me in the back of his car.

"Worth it," I muttered to myself as he slammed the door.

***

I'd never been arrested before, but if I was expecting a dark and dank jail cell, I was disappointed. The jail, which was attached to the police station and right next door to the municipal office, was surprisingly clean and smelled of the cinnamon apple plug-in by the door.

Sitting on the bench, I leaned my head back against the wall, absently rubbing at the bruises that were already forming on my wrists and my arm where Murphy had squeezed me harder than necessary. I'd only been there thirty minutes or so, but I'd already gotten to make my one phone call.

Not knowing how Dad would take my arrest, I'd called Aunt Gracie instead. She was the club's defense attorney, as well as Uncle Hawk's wife. I asked her not to tell my parents I was in jail, but I was pretty sure my uncle was listening in, and I doubted he would keep this from either of them.

The thick door separating the cells from the rest of the station was suddenly yanked open so hard, it banged off the wall. I cringed, expecting Dad, but when I looked up, it was to see a raging bull storming toward me.

I clenched my hands into fists, but I kept my face neutral as Ben used a set of keys to unlock my cell. Leaving the door open, he crouched down in front of me and carefully grasped my wrists, examining them. When he saw the bruises on them, the fire in his eyes spiked higher.

"Are you okay?" he asked in a voice that sounded choked.

"I'm fine," I gritted out, jerking away from his touch.

He closed his eyes as if he were in pain, but I couldn't handle being so close to him without wanting to punch him in the face. Standing, I walked to the other side of the cell and turned to face him.

"Lexa, let me explain," he pleaded as he straightened. "Paige—"

"No," I told him in a voice devoid of all emotion, while inside, everything was a blaze of pure chaos. "I don't want to hear about Paige. I don't want to hear anything you have to say, actually. Whatever your excuses are, save them. This game is over, and I'm not playing anymore."

"Baby, this isn't a game. Paige and I—"

"No!" I screamed, turning away from him. "Just leave me alone, Ben."

"You have every right to be upset, but just listen to me," he commanded, holding his hands up in a way he must have thought would calm me.

It didn't. The calm I'd felt earlier while destroying his work vehicle was gone now that I was face-to-face with him. The pain had returned, along with the anger.

"Hey, Deputy!" I yelled, knowing that asshole Murphy could hear me with the door wide open now. "Where the fuck is my lawyer?"

"Lexa." Ben was only a foot away now and slowly closing in on me, as if he were afraid I would bolt if he didn't approach cautiously.

With the cell door wide open, I could have made a run for it, but there was the chance they would charge me with attempting to escape.

"Baby, I swear to you, Paige and I aren't together. If you saw her kissing me…" His voice faded when I turned my hate-filled gaze on him.

"If?" I seethed, stepping into his space. "If I saw you two kissing? Wasn't that your plan, Sheriff? For me to show up like some love-sick fool and find you mouth-fucking your ex? That was the whole point in giving me a key, right? So I could walk right in and you could play your sick game a little more? It doesn't happen often, but you really played me. Congratulations. You've done what no one else in this shit town ever could before. Are you satisfied? Does it make you feel good to know you got so close and were able to make the frigid ice princess melt in the palm of your hand?"

"You're so damn stubborn," he growled, cupping my elbows in his hands. His large fingers brushed over the bruise on the upper part of my forearm, and I couldn't hide the wince of pain it caused me.

Ben saw it and lifted my arm to inspect it closer. When he saw the fingerprint-shaped bruises already darkening my skin, his nostrils flared. "I'll fucking kill him."

"Go ahead. I'll just wait right here." I pulled from his grasp, walking away from him again.

The sound of heels on the tiled floor had us both turning to watch as Aunt Gracie walked through the door. Dressed in jeans, a plain gray T-shirt, and heeled sandals, she looked like she was closer to my age. She had genes that only made her more beautiful with age. Her hellion of a son hadn't even added a single gray hair or line to her ageless face.

Seeing my cell was open, she lifted her brows and turned the full force of her professional glare on him. Ben straightened his spine, and I felt my lips twitch with the beginnings of a grin. Aunt Gracie was one of the sweetest women I'd ever met, but when she was doing her job, she was a tigress on the hunt.

"Can I go home now?" I asked her hopefully as I walked over to the bars.

"Hawk is posting your bail," she assured me. "You can go as soon as that's taken care of."

"She wouldn't even have to post bail if Murphy had come in and told me what was going on," Ben said as he came to stand behind me. "She never would have been arrested."

"Yet, she was," my aunt said with a skeptical raise of her brows. "And just what were you doing, Sheriff, while my niece was being arrested? The incident happened right outside your apartment. Are you telling me you didn't hear anything that would make you suspect someone was being so roughly apprehended?"

I didn't want to see the look on his face while she questioned him. I put more distance between us, hating that I could feel his heat radiating against my back. But even when I put the width of the cell in between us, I could still feel him like he was physically touching me.

"I was dealing with a personal issue at the time and was distracted. When I was walking Paige out, I saw Lexa's car and the engine was on. Then I saw the damage done to the cruiser and realized something had happened."

I rolled my eyes at Aunt Gracie when she glanced my way, but I shrugged when she seemed to be waiting for an explanation from me. "What the sheriff means is that he was so busy with his tongue down his ex's throat, he wouldn't have heard a bomb going off, let alone someone happening to take a bat to his precious cruiser."

"It wasn't like that, goddamn it!" he snapped at me, frustration flooding off him in waves, and I took a sick pleasure in knowing I was tying him in knots.

"I think I should speak to my client alone, Sheriff," Aunt Gracie informed him, stepping back and holding her hand out toward the door that led to the front of the police station, indicating for him to leave.

"If I could drop the charges, I would," he told me, his tone imploring me to believe him. "But Campbell already found out, and because it was county property, I have no say over what happens next."

"Don't sweat it. I knew what kind of trouble I was going to get into when I did what I did."

"What she allegedly did," Aunt Gracie was quick to correct. "Other than Officer Murphy's word, there is no solid evidence that she was responsible for what happened to the cruiser. And given the state Lexa is currently in, with scratches on her face and bruises on her arms and wrists, I don't think he is a credible witness, given his mistreatment of my client."

Ben's jaw turned to stone. "He'll pay for this, believe that."

"I suggest you keep your hands clean, Sheriff Davis," she instructed. "I'm sure the deputy regrets his actions."

I bit my lip to keep from laughing, knowing she figured my dad and uncles would take care of Murphy themselves. I might have felt bad for the poor man if my body weren't aching so badly from how roughly he'd handled me earlier.

"He's going to be begging for his mommy when I get done with him," Ben muttered as he walked out, the door slamming behind him.

With the sheriff now gone, Aunt Gracie walked into the cell with me. "Are you okay? You look like hell, honey."

"I put up a little bit of a fight when Murphy arrested me. I don't think there is a single part of me that doesn't ache right now." Rubbing at my sore wrists, I sat down on the bench, too tired to continue to stand around. Who knew how long it would take for my uncle to post my bail.

"Do you want to tell me what happened?"

"I thought if you knew the truth, you couldn't defend me?" I asked with a tiny smile.

"Let's take a time-out from me being your lawyer and just let me be your aunt for a moment. I can turn off the professional side of my head and forget anything you happen to say to incriminate yourself while in family mode." Sitting beside me, she crossed her legs as she half turned to face me. "Were you and Davis dating?"

"Nope. He was just playing a game with me." I felt my face heat with embarrassment at having to admit that out loud. A lump filled my throat, and I had to swallow hard a few times before it would go away. "I saw him earlier today, and he convinced me to come over tonight to talk. After asking Mom if she was okay with it, I decided to go. But..." Tears burned my eyes, and I lowered my lashes so she couldn't witness just how gullible I'd been. "But when I showed up, the door was already ajar, and he was... He..."

Soft hands pulled my head down to her chest, and I couldn't hold back the sob a second longer. "Okay, okay. Shh, it's all right. I get the picture."

"H-he played me," I said with a whimper. "I was so s-st-stupid."

"Guys are douchebags, honey. Not your uncle, of course, but at least ninety-eight percent of the male population is." She rubbed one hand down my back, trying to comfort me. "Don't worry about the bastard sheriff. You can do so much better."

"I just want to go home," I whispered against her shirt.

"I don't know if you want to do that just yet," she murmured, looking down at me with a guilty tinge to her cheeks. "Hawk called your dad. He's not all that happy right now."

A snort left me, and even though the tears were still spilling, I found myself laughing. "I bet. But I don't care if Dad is mad or not. I just want a shower and to go to bed."

She started to say something, but her phone chimed with a text message just as the door leading to the station opened again. Ben walked back in, his face grim as he approached my cell.

Aunt Gracie stood. "Hawk is waiting for us out front. Come on, we'll drop you off on our way."

By the time we got to the cell door, Ben was standing there waiting. "Baby, let me drive you home," he said imploringly. "We need to talk."

Scrubbing my hands over my still damp cheeks, I shook my head. Keeping my gaze on the wall over his shoulder, I refused to meet his eyes, too embarrassed to let him see just how much pain I was in. "I have nothing left to say to you. And anything you want to say to me, I seriously don't want to hear."

Muttering a curse, he took two steps toward me. I took three steps back, knowing if he touched me, I was going to start crying all over again. He kept coming, and I kept backing up until I connected with the cell's wall. "Campbell is ruining my life," he muttered, so low I barely heard him even as close as he was. "Everything that is going on with Paige and me is because of him. Nothing else. I swear to you."

"Forgive me if I don't believe you," I gritted out between clenched teeth, trying and failing to keep my emotions in check. "My father told me he wouldn't stand in my way if I wanted to be with you. He also told me you needed to respect my decision if I decided you weren't what I wanted. Well, I don't want you, Ben. Now leave me the hell alone."

Brushing past him, I took the hand Aunt Gracie offered and clung to it as we walked away, the first tears falling before we even made it to the door.

T HIRT EEN

As the door shut behind Lexa and her aunt, I couldn't hold back the rage-filled bellow demanding to be set free. My fist connected with the cell wall, and I pounded out my frustration and anger until I couldn't feel my hand anymore.

This shit was getting out of hand, and I was losing control not only of the situation, but I was losing Lexa too.

Blood dripped from my knuckles, red droplets sprinkling over the stark-white wall. The pain in my hand did nothing to calm the beast wanting to be unleashed on the world right then, though.

As badly as I'd wanted Lexa to come home from New York, part of me wished she'd stayed a little longer. Then none of this would have happened. Paige would have been gone by next week, the investigation would have been over, and Campbell would have been out of all our hair.

The week before, when Paige showed up out of the blue, telling me she was going to help with the investigation into Campbell, I'd been pissed. She did plenty of work for her father, but I didn't want her sticking her nose in this. I thought the attorney general would have picked someone from Creswell Springs so as not to draw attention to a newcomer. This town was too small for a newbie not to stick out like a sore thumb.

As I suspected, the second Paige stepped into the municipal office, Campbell smelled blood. To divert his attention, we decided to let everyone think Paige moved to town because we were trying to get back together, but Campbell hadn't bought that at first. I still wasn't sure he had. And now that Lexa was back, I didn't think I could keep up the pretense.

What happened earlier only proved that I couldn't.

Paige had shown up at my door trembling because she thought Campbell or someone else was following her. To throw him off the scent, when I'd heard someone at the door, I'd pulled her in for a kiss, thinking it was Campbell spying on the two of us.

Fuck, I'd gotten it wrong.

Since Lexa hadn't shown up at eight, I figured she was just being stubborn and wasn't going to come like I'd asked her to. I didn't imagine it was her at the door and that she saw me kissing someone else. Now I might have fucked up everything with her completely.

Walking through the police station, I shot Murphy a glare as I passed him. I'd bitched him out earlier, but there were too many cameras and witnesses around for me to do to him what I really wanted to do. I suspected Campbell had someone in his pocket, and if I had to take a guess, Murphy would be at the top of that list. He was a little weasel, but I'd deal with him very, very soon.

When I got to the parking lot, Hawk Hannigan's car was pulling out into traffic. Jogging over to my truck, I jumped in and followed them.

Ten minutes later, the car pulled into Lexa's driveway, and Hawk and Gracie both got out.

Before they reached the front door, it opened and Bash stepped out. I put my truck in park and turned off the engine, but I didn't follow after them. Instead, I leaned back in my seat, getting comfortable.

As I watched, Hawk and Gracie spoke to Bash for a few minutes while Lexa stood there with her arms crossed, mutinously saying nothing. From the porch light, I could see Bash was anything but happy, but he wasn't raging at Lexa. Still, I kept my eyes on him in case he made a sudden move.

Eventually, the Hannigans said goodnight, and they both hugged Lexa before going back to their car. Bash turned to Lexa, pulled her hard against him for a hug. After only a small hesitation, Lexa hugged him back, and they walked into the house with their arms still around each other.

Hawk backed out of the driveway, and as he passed me, he threw up his hand in acknowledgment.

I waited for over an hour until all the lights were turned off inside the house, keeping my eyes glued to the second-story window I knew was Lexa's bedroom. During that time, my hand started to swell and the bleeding continued. I had a box of Kleenex in my glove box that I used to make a bandage, but I knew I probably needed stitches to close a few of the deep gashes on my knuckles.

It could wait, though.

Once her light was out, I waited another thirty minutes before getting out and quietly shutting my door. While I'd been sitting in my truck, I'd mapped out how best to get inside the house. Using the banister on the porch, I climbed up to the roof and then walked around to the side of the house with Lexa's window.

I wasn't surprised to find the window unlocked. Not many people locked their second-story windows. I wanted to scold Lexa for not being safe, but at the same time, I was thankful she'd made it easier for me to get to her.

Silently, I climbed into her bedroom and closed the window. The room was in complete darkness, and it took a few seconds for my eyes to adjust. When I could see the outline of her bed, I crossed to it. Kicking off my shoes, I climbed in beside her.

Only when my arms were around her did the rage monster inside me start to calm down. Pressing my face into her hair, I inhaled deeply, needing her scent to fill me.

Lexa startled awake, and I quickly covered her mouth to keep her from screaming and alerting her father to my presence. Whatever truce we'd called when I'd confided in him about my plans for Campbell, I doubted extended to finding me in his daughter's bed.

Her eyes widened in fear until I stroked a hand down her spine. "Shh, it's me, beautiful."

The fear turned to anger, and she spat muffled curses at me against my hand.

"You are so damn stubborn. I knew this was the only way to make you listen." My hand trailed down her back and over her luscious ass, pressing her lower body against my own. Fuck, but she felt good. She was wearing some old shirt that felt thin and had a few holes in it, making me remember I needed to give her one of my own for her to sleep in. But first, I had to get her to understand there was nothing going on between Paige and me.

Leaning in closer, I breathed in her scent again, savoring it. "I called in a favor, and

Campbell is now under investigation by the state's attorney general. It's a secret investigation, but the AG sent Paige, his daughter, to head it up. Campbell is smart, and he sensed something off the second he set eyes on her. We've been letting everyone think she's only in town because she wants to get back together with me. Tonight, on her way home from work, she thought Campbell or someone who works for him was following her. I thought it was him at the door, and that's why I kissed Paige, to make it look more convincing. I swear, that's the only time I've kissed her since she's been here. Nothing else has happened between us, and nothing else will."

She said something against my mouth, but I didn't understand and cautiously lifted my hand to let her repeat it.

"I don't believe you," she whispered, pushing at my chest, but I wasn't going anywhere, so she couldn't budge me. "Maybe about the Campbell thing, sure, but not about Paige. Your ex shows up, and suddenly, you have to pretend like you're in a relationship again? Then out of the blue, she's at your door—conveniently at the same time I'm supposed to show up so we can talk—and you need to kiss her? That's bullshit, Ben. Either you're playing me, or she's playing you. Whatever it is, I'm not going to be pulled into your games with your ex."

My hand clenched at her hip, and I pressed my forehead to hers. "Baby, I don't want Paige. Whatever was between us burned out a long time ago. I'm just trying to keep her safe until we can get Campbell out of our hair once and for all."

"It might have burned out on your side, but hers still seems to be blazing," she mumbled with what sounded like a pout in her voice.

"If it is, that's on her. The only woman I want is you. Can't you feel how badly, baby?" I thrust my hips forward. Her thighs opened ever so slightly, and I felt her shirt rise an inch. My hand moved down to push it up even farther, and I felt the little scrap of cotton that was covering her pussy and the dampness already coating the insides of her soft thighs. "I ache for you," I breathed in her ear and felt her shudder.

"N-no," she said in a voice that was weak with the same need that was burning my blood. "I won't give in to you again... Oh God. Ben, that feels good."

Nipping at her neck, I cupped her pussy through her panties, my thumb playing with her slit. "This is the only way I would ever play with you, beautiful," I rasped in her ear. "I'll gladly tease and torment you until you beg me to let you come on my fingers. But I will never play games with your heart. Not when I want it more than I want inside this sweet pussy."

"Ben," she moaned, willingly spreading her thighs wider, granting me full access to utopia.

Smothering a groan against her neck, I shoved the panties down her legs. She mewled a protest when my hand left her, but as soon as she was free of the little piece of cotton, I spread her lips and skimmed my middle finger over her clit.

Her entire body trembled at the first caress, her hands clenching in my shirt. When I felt how wet and ready she was for me already, my dick leaked onto my thigh, screaming for attention. But I didn't come here to get off. I came to show her she could trust me, and if I had to, to beg for a little time to clean up the mess I'd created when I'd tried to get that bastard Campbell out of our lives so we could be together.

But I'd be damned if I was leaving before she came all over my fingers. I needed to feel her lose control for me, and I needed to show her that she would always be my top priority.

"You smell like heaven," I told her as I circled her opening. "I want to bury my face right here." I thrust one finger into her and nearly came in my jeans at how tight she was. "And lick up all this honey."

"Please," she whimpered, pressing her face into my chest to muffle the achy little sounds she couldn't control.

"Tell me this is my pussy," I commanded, playing with her clit while thrusting one digit in and out of her tight heat. "Tell me you're mine, Lexa."

"I…" She shook her head. "No. I'm not yours."

Growling, I took my thumb away from her clit but kept thrusting my finger into her. "You are. Your body, your heart, your soul. They are all mine. Tell me, and I'll make you feel so good, baby."

"You can have my body, but not my heart."

Clenching my jaw, I pulled my finger from her and thrust two into her, stretching her a little more. "I want it all," I told her greedily. "Tell me, Lexa. Give me what I want."

"N-no." She shook her head stubbornly. "I won't give you anything else to hurt me with." Grabbing my wrist, she pulled back enough so that our eyes locked in the darkness. "Take what I'm offering—or leave. I'll just get myself off when you're gone."

"Will you now?" Grinning, I propped myself up on one arm, looking down at her. "Show me."

"Ben!" she hissed.

"I'm serious. Show me how you make yourself come. Do you rub your perfect little pussy with your fingers? Or maybe you have a toy. If I looked in your nightstand drawer, would I find a vibrator, baby?" She looked away, but I caught her chin between my thumb and index finger, turning her face back toward me. "Show me. I want to see you touch yourself."

"The vibrator is in the nightstand behind you," she informed me, giving in.

I grabbed it from the drawer. The little egg-shaped thing was swallowed by my hand, but it fit perfectly in hers. Rolling onto her back, she pulled her sleep shirt up to her stomach, exposing her bare pussy.

I wanted to turn on the light so I could see her better, but I knew it would only draw attention if someone got up.

Keeping her eyes on me, she turned on the little egg and then rubbed it down her flat stomach and straight to her clit. The tiny gasp that left her when it first made contact had me rubbing my palm over my cock, trying to ease some of the pressure already building in my balls.

Her lashes started to lower. "Eyes on me," I ordered, and they flicked upward once more.

Getting on my knees, I moved between her spread thighs, needing to see it all. "Lift your shirt," I instructed.

Without hesitation, she lifted her shirt with her free hand until both her tits were exposed. Cupping one in her palm, she lifted it toward me in offer, but I shook my head. "Play with your nipples for me."

As she pinched and tugged on first one nipple, then the other, I heard her pussy getting wetter and sucked my fingers I'd had in her moments before, licking her essence from each digit.

"Ah," she whimpered. "I'm close."

I fell on her then, pushing the vibrator out of my way and sucking her clit into my mouth. I flicked it with my tongue, drowning in the honey that flooded from her as I tried to lick it all up. She fisted her hands in my hair, lifting her hips off the mattress as she rode my face until she was coming apart on my tongue.

I pressed my hips into the bed and sucked her clit even harder to keep from shouting as my own release hit me with the force of a tsunami, and I shot load after load in my boxer briefs and jeans.

When I found the energy to sit up, we were both still breathing hard, and I wiped her remaining juices off my face. She looked up at me sleepily, and I lay down beside her, cuddling her for a little longer before I had to leave. I didn't want to give Bash a reason to shoot me, so I knew I had to go before long or risk him finding me in Lexa's bed.

Trustingly, she put her head on my chest and wrapped her arm over my stomach. Kissing the top of her head, I savored the peace that filled me in that moment.

It was only a matter of minutes before her breathing evened out and she was fast asleep. Wishing I could stay like this with her forever, I gave myself another half an hour before carefully untangling our bodies and then tucking the covers back over her.

As I was putting my boots back on, I noticed her phone charging on the nightstand and picked it up. Surprisingly, there wasn't a lock code, so I went in and unblocked my number, knowing she was too stubborn to do it herself.

Grinning, I started to replace it, when I saw she had a text message alert. The grin disappeared when I clicked on it and saw it was from some guy named Theo. I read the last text he sent.

Theo: If you need me, I'm there. Just say the word. Call me when you get up. I want to hear your voice so I know for sure you're okay.

I didn't like how this Theo guy seemed to be so close to her. Feeling the rage monster in me start to rear his head, I thumbed up, seeing how far back the texts went. It went as far back as two weeks before not letting me see anything else, and I started reading again.

From what I read, they met up in New York and, from the looks of it, spent a lot of time together. There was a lot of joking about how Theo's mom wouldn't take no for an answer and kept buying Lexa things, and Lexa begging him to save her from his mother and aunt. There were plans for dinners and even a movie date. He was the one to drive her to the airport the day she came home, and he'd said he missed her already that same night.

My hand clenched around the phone, and I heard it creak at the mistreatment. My knuckles protested the tightening of muscles, the gashes that had started to seal and scab over opening again, causing blood to drip down my fingers.

Gritting my teeth, I blocked Theo's number and then erased his text history, along with his contact information. I didn't know who this guy was to Lexa, but I wasn't taking any chances with him wanting what was mine.

FOURTEEN

A tap on my door pulled me from the most peaceful sleep I'd had in what felt like forever. Frowning, I reached for my phone to see what time it was just as the door opened and Aunt Flick stuck her head around.

"You okay?" she asked in a quiet voice as I sat up, pushing my sleep-tousled hair out of my face with one hand and holding the blanket tucked under my arms to hide my nakedness.

Seeing it was only just after seven, I nodded. "I'm good."

The lights were still off, but as she walked farther into the room, she flipped the switch. "Lexa!" she gasped, shutting the door and running across the room to touch my cheek. "What the hell happened?"

I winced at her gentle touch grazing my tender cheek, right beside my scar. "You mean the entire world doesn't already know?" I tried to joke, only to get a stern look from her. Sighing heavily, I told her about being arrested. "Murphy was pretty rough with me last night. My entire body was aching when I got home, but it's worse now. I feel like I got hit by a bus."

She was already examining my arms and wrists, her eyes on fire. Looking up at me, she finally realized I wasn't wearing any clothes. "Lexa…"

Blushing, I pulled the covers closer. "It was really hot last night," I muttered.

She rolled her eyes. "Relax, I'm not going to say anything to your parents. Neither one of them can really say anything, if you ask me. Not with how Bash was always sneaking in to Raven's room to spend the night. Just be careful, honey. If either he or Jet find him sneaking in here, he's a dead man."

Standing, she shook her head when her blue eyes fell on my cheek. "Your mom is going to burn the police station down to get to Murphy when she sees you. I almost feel sorry for the bastard. Almost."

I already knew that, which was why I wasn't looking forward to seeing her.

Hand on the doorknob, Aunt Flick suddenly turned back to face me. "Right, the reason I came in here in the first place. Theo Volkov called me a few minutes ago. He said all his texts to you keep not delivering. Thought something was wrong with you. I see you're alive and mostly well, but you should check on why your phone is blocking your friend."

Promising her I would, I waited for her to close the door before pulling up my texts.

Only to find Theo's text feed wasn't there. Frowning, I pulled up my contacts, but Theo wasn't there either.

"Damn it, Ben!" I whisper-shouted to myself.

Luckily, I remember Theo's number and added the contact information back. But when I tried to text him, I quickly realized I needed to unblock his number. Angry that Ben had been looking through my phone and deleted my best friend from it, I sent a text to Theo assuring him I was fine before pulling up Ben's contact.

As I'd expected, his number was already unblocked, and I hit connect, waiting impatiently for him to answer.

"Good morning, beautiful," his deep voice purred in my ear. "Did you sleep well?"

"Stay the hell out of my phone!" I raged in as quiet a voice as I could while still getting the point across. "You had no business erasing Theo's information from my contacts."

"Who is this guy anyway?" he asked, his voice immediately losing the purr.

"He's none of your damn business. We aren't together, and even if we were, you had no right even looking at my phone, let alone blocking and deleting people from it."

"I'll concede to the phone thing. That was a mistake on my part. My only excuse is that I was jealous...*am* jealous of this Theo idiot. I'll try not to let it get the better of me again. But you're wrong about us not being together. You came all over my face last night, baby."

Heat filled my face, a mixture of embarrassment and remembered need that was suddenly making my body ache for a reason other than Murphy's rough treatment. As I glanced at the window, a piece of me hoped I would see him on the other side, ready to come in and take care of the throb deep between my thighs once again.

Red fingerprints on the window frame caught my attention, distracting me completely from the naughty thoughts of Ben's mouth on my pussy. Was that…blood?

"Ben," I whispered as I jumped out of bed and rushed over to the window, examining the stains. "Were you bleeding last night?"

"I might have had to go to the emergency room after I left you this morning for some stitches," he informed me, his tone making it seem like it wasn't important.

"What?" I exclaimed, feeling dizzy all of a sudden. "Are you okay?"

"I'm fine."

"But why did you need stitches?" I demanded. "Did you come here bleeding, and I didn't even realize?"

"I busted my knuckles last night," he hedged.

"On Murphy's face?" Oh Lord, he was going to lose his job because of me. I dropped down on the edge of my bed, putting my face in my free hand.

"No, baby. I haven't had the chance to deal with that… It's nothing. Just a few stitches in three of my knuckles. It happened before I came over last night. Don't worry about me. How are you feeling? Do the bruises hurt?"

"I'm fine," I gritted out, knowing he wasn't telling me what happened on purpose. If he wanted to be in a relationship with me, he needed to be honest. Even about the small things.

But this wasn't small.

He'd gotten hurt somehow the night before and wasn't telling me how.

"I have to go," I told him, already back on my feet and walking into the bathroom to get the Windex to clean up the blood smears. If Dad or Mom came in and saw the blood, they would freak, and Mom would check my body from head to toe for life-threatening injuries.

"Lexa, don't be mad," he tried to soothe.

"I'm not mad," I assured him, fighting tears for some reason. "Just disappointed that you aren't being honest with me. Guess we aren't together after all if you can't even tell me what happened that would require you having to get stitches. But whatever."

"I punched a damn wall last night, okay?" he growled. "I didn't want you to know that I... Hell, I get these moments when I can't control the rage that seems to live inside me, Lexa. Last night, I lost control and punched the wall and split my knuckles open."

"Why didn't you just say that?" I demanded.

"Because I didn't want to scare you or make you think you have to worry about me ever losing control with you. I would never hurt you, baby. Never."

The anger draining from me, I closed my eyes. "It would take a hell of a lot more than you punching a wall to scare me, Ben. I've seen some evil things in my lifetime. You're not evil. Rage or no rage, I feel safe when I'm with you."

"Good, because I would kill anyone who tried to hurt you."

"I know that," I told him softly.

"Lexa..." He broke off, and I heard a voice in the background. A female voice. "Hold on, baby," he told me before his voice and the female's became muffled. I knew then exactly who was talking to him.

Paige.

Fuck, I'd completely forgotten about her.

Ben could so easily make me forget everything but him and me, it was crazy. I didn't understand how he could make me block out everything that didn't revolve around the two of us being together, but he did, and I hated it.

With each passing second he made me wait, my jealousy only grew. I cleaned up his bloody fingerprints and then made sure there weren't any other signs he'd been there the night before. I didn't even remember him leaving. Of course, he'd put me in a postorgasmic coma, so it was all his fault I'd passed out and didn't hear him.

While I waited, Theo texted me back.

Theo: Are you sure you don't need me?

"Lexa?" Ben's voice filled my ear once again. "Something just came up, baby. I want to see you later. Have dinner with me tonight."

"No thanks," I told him coolly.

"Lexa," he growled.

"I already have plans for this evening, actually." Not a lie. I did have plans. They just involved an accounts book for Hannigans'. "Have a great day, Sheriff. I'm sure it will be now that your ex is in your office."

"Don't be jealous, beautiful," he murmured in that purr again, but I wasn't going to fall under his spell again. "I swear, this will all be over soon, and she'll be gone."

"How sad for you. Then you won't have anyone to play with." Another text from Theo came in and I grinned. "Ah, would you look at that? Gotta go. Theo is so sweet. Offering to fly all this way just to hold my hand."

"Lexa." There was pure malicious rage in his voice now, and it only made my grin bigger. "Don't play with me."

"I'm not the one who plays games, Sheriff. That would be you. I have the text right here in front of me with him asking if I need him, and he'll be on the first flight out if I do. Should I screenshot it and send you the picture? Hmm, maybe I should take him up on his offer. He could keep me company while you wrap everything up with Paige." I tapped my chin with my index finger, pretending to give the idea some serious thought, but I knew I wouldn't ever let Theo leave his family even if I did feel like I needed someone in my corner. Ben's reaction to the thought of someone else in my life was plenty enough satisfaction for me.

"Lexa," he snapped, and I had to swallow a laugh. "I'll see you tonight. We'll discuss this more then."

"As I said, I have plans for the evening. And they don't include you. Stay safe, Sheriff. I heard there's someone crazy chick going around taking baseball bats to police cruisers."

"Lexa, I swear, you're so damn stubborn. You're going to give me an ulcer or something. I'll see you tonight."

"No. You. Won't." Satisfied I'd had the last word, I hung up and stomped into the bathroom.

It was only when I caught sight of my nakedness in the mirror that I remembered I wasn't wearing any clothes. I couldn't believe I'd just had that entire conversation nude. Even if he couldn't see me, it was unlike me. My scar had always made me too self-conscious about the rest of my body, not just my face. Yet, I completely forgot while I was on the phone with him.

Turning on the shower, I nearly groaned when I received a new text.

Ben: See. You. Tonight. And tell Theo you don't need him for anything. You have me.

Before I could type out a reply, another one popped up.

Ben: Your car is parked in front of your house. I dropped it off on my way to work this morning. Drive safely if you need to go anywhere.

Ben: PS. I miss you.

FIFTEEN

Walking into the kitchen an hour later, I was surprised to find Mom chopping vegetables while Uncle Jet stood close by, drinking his morning coffee and looking all out of humor.

"Morning, honey," Mom greeted, barely lifting her head from her task. "I'm so glad you're up. I was hoping you could run to the grocery store for me and grab a few things for this chili I'm mak…ing."

When she finally got a good look at me, the knife dropped out of her hand, clanging loudly against the countertop. She was in front of me before I even realized she was in motion, worrying me with how fast she'd moved in case she hurt herself.

Fingers trembling, she skimmed them over my cheek, and I did my best not to flinch. Tears filled her eyes as she quickly took stock of the rest of my body that she could see. When she lifted my arms and examined the bruises, the tears dried instantaneously and flames flashed in her green depths.

"Who?"

One word. That was all she said, but it was enough.

No "what" or "when." Just "who." All I had to say was Murphy's name, and I knew he would breathe his last breath while she watched. And just knowing she would kill anyone who harmed me had my throat tightening with emotion, but I wouldn't supply the name, wouldn't be the one responsible for a man's death and risk Mom losing her freedom.

"So…" I cleared my throat, trying to lace my voice with amusement. "I was kind of arrested last night. Long story. I might have caused some county property damage by taking a baseball bat to the sheriff's work cruiser. In the process of getting arrested, I struggled, and this was the aftermath. No biggie."

"Davis did this to you?" she seethed.

Panic that she was now planning Ben's death had me quickly shaking my head. "No, no, no, Mom. Ben didn't arrest me. It was Mur—" I broke off before I could finish the name, but the damage had already been done.

"Murphy?" she guessed. "Does your dad know anything about all this?"

"Yup," Jet supplied from where he was still leaning against the sink, sipping his coffee calmly like his baby sister wasn't about to explode with rage.

"And Murphy is still breathing?" she gritted out between clenched teeth.

"As far as I know." He shrugged his shoulders, but Mom's gaze was locked on the scrapes on my cheek and didn't see him.

"Our daughter is arrested, harmed by some pussy Barney Fife wannabe, and he doesn't tell me? What the hell else has he kept from me?" She touched my cheek again, and when I couldn't hide my flinch this time, her tears returned. "Baby, I'm so sorry. I haven't been around for you enough lately. Please forgive me."

My eyes widened. "Mom, what are you talking about? You're always here for me."

Two fat tears fell down her cheeks, and she shook her head. "No. You've been going through so much lately, and I've been so caught up in this damn cancer thing, I've lost track of everything going on in your and your brother's lives."

She enfolded me in her arms, hugging me so tight I struggled to breathe for a few moments, but I hugged her back. Her tears were making my own rush to the surface, and all I wanted to do was comfort her.

"Who am I killing, Rave?" Uncle Jet asked casually, putting his now-empty mug in the sink. "Murphy or Bash?"

Mom gave me one last squeeze before walking back over to the chopping board. "No one," she answered just as casually, and I shuddered. "If you touch either of them, I'm going to be pissed."

"Raven—"

"I said no," she barked. "I'll deal with Bash and Murphy myself."

"But you're supposed to be taking it easy." She turned her head, giving him a look that had him shutting his mouth with a snap. They had a staredown, and I was seriously getting nervous when Mom returned to chopping the vegetables. "Lexa, do you feel up to going to the grocery store for me?"

"Sure, Mom." Anything to get out of there. Mom was making me nervous as hell. "Do you have a list?"

She motioned with the knife to a Post-it on the fridge. "I think that's all I need. Your brother mentioned wanting chili yesterday, and I woke up craving it."

"Where is Max anyway?"

"He went to work with your dad this morning. Dad was pissed at him for some reason." She narrowed her eyes on me. "Do you know anything about that?"

"Mom, it's Max we're talking about. Dad could have been pissed at him for a hundred different reasons," I reminded her, but I couldn't help wondering if Dad was punishing Max for what he'd said to me about Mom. That still stung, but I wasn't going to narc on my little brother.

Mom was already unpredictable, and I didn't want to risk Max losing a limb for a moment of idiocy.

Grabbing the list off the fridge, I called a "bye" as I headed out. As Ben's text said, my car was parked at the end of the driveway. My purse was still in the front seat, I saw as I got in. When I started it, I immediately noticed two things.

I had a full tank of gas. There had been a quarter of a tank when I'd driven over to Ben's apartment the night before, but it was completely full now.

And there was a huge shirt folded under my purse that I could already tell smelled just like Ben. Grabbing it, I lifted it to my nose, inhaling deeply. I fell asleep with that scent filling my senses the night before, his arms wrapped around me, making me feel like there wasn't a force in the world that could touch or harm me as long as he was right there holding me.

Pulling out my phone, I texted Ben.

Me: Thanks for the shirt and the gas.

Smiling to myself, I drove to the grocery store. As soon as I walked through the automatic doors, however, the smile disappeared as all eyes turned in my direction.

I realized then I was the headlining topic of gossip for the entire town that morning.

Gritting my teeth, I got a basket and quickly grabbed all the things on Mom's list. The last item on the list was sliced cheese from the deli. Mom loved thick slices for grilled cheese with soup and chili, and my stomach growled at the thought of a bowl with the gooey melted cheese sandwiches, reminding me I hadn't eaten breakfast yet.

There were two people already in line, both of them older women. Standing back at a respectable distance, I waited for them to finish ordering. The first lady was ordering the entire deli, it seemed, so I pulled out my phone to distract myself while waiting.

Seeing I had a reply to my earlier text, I opened it, my smile returning.

Ben: Wear it every night and dream of me.

"...can't believe she did that to his vehicle," the woman in front of me was saying, pulling my attention from my phone to her.

I narrowed my gaze on the woman even as I felt my cheeks heat.

"I'm not worried about it," the first woman assured the second, her focus on the selection of deli meats while the attendant behind the counter sliced up her Cajun turkey. "I know he's just trying to give Paige a hard time with that Reid girl until he finally forgives her and takes her back."

Every muscle in my body tensed, and I took a closer look at the first woman. After a moment, I realized who she was and felt my stomach bottom out.

Hannah Davis.

Ben's grandmother.

"I mean, seriously, I know my grandson," she said without turning. "He was miserable after breaking up with Paige. That was why he came back to Creswell Springs in the first place. To start over. He's on top of the world now that she's back."

Suddenly, I was glad I hadn't eaten yet, because I knew I would have vomited then and there if I had.

"I like the Reid family, don't get me wrong. That Sebastian does one heck of a job on my car every time I need something done to it, and he is always so cordial. And Raven is a decent girl. I hate that she's going through so much with her health right now. But their daughter… Well, she's not exactly who I would want my only grandchild to be with. Look how unstable she is. Taking a bat to a vehicle with or without provocation tells me right there how crazy she is. Just like her biological mother, if you ask me. I heard she was..."

Her voice trailed off as she turned to look at the woman behind her and finally noticed me standing in line.

All the blood drained from her face, and I figured it only matched my own. My hands felt ice cold as I clenched them around the handle of the basket and my phone. Only a minute before, I'd been smiling down at my phone like a fool, happy, even though I was embarrassed as hell to be out in public after my actions the night before.

Now, all that happiness had drained away, and I realized how crazy I really was. Crazy to think Ben and I stood a chance.

"Close your mouth, Mrs. Davis," a voice I knew and loved commanded as I felt a soft hand touch my back. "You've more than said your two cents. Now it's my turn."

I grabbed Aunt Willa's arm when she took a step in the old woman's direction, stopping whatever she was about to do. Blinking back tears, I cleared my throat. "No. It's okay. She's entitled to her opinion. And as she said, she knows her grandson. Of course he's only playing with me to make his ex jealous."

"I… That's not what I meant, actually." Flustered, she took a step forward, but I took two steps back. "Lexa dear, I'm so sorry. I didn't mean—"

"Oh, I think you did, ma'am," Aunt Willa assured her. "Why else would you say it?"

"Because…" Grimacing, she wrung her hands together. "Because I'm an old fool who likes to gossip."

"Glad to see you can admit it. But you've made your opinion on the subject loud and clear." Aunt Willa stepped in front of me, her eyes darkening like storm clouds when she saw the scratch on my cheek, but she didn't comment on it. "What do you need here, sweetheart? I'll grab it and drop it off on my way home."

"Ch-cheese," I muttered, my voice weak. I hated it, but I was so close to tears, I couldn't really see her face. "Two pounds of the Colby-Jack sliced extra thick."

She smiled. "Raven must be making chili."

I nodded, swallowing the lump in my throat.

"You go on and check out. I'll get the cheese." I let her turn me toward the front of the store, not looking back when her hand dropped from my back. Blindly, I checked out and walked to my car, feeling defeated.

SIXTEEN

Paige shifted uneasily in the chair in front of my desk as I put my phone away after texting Lexa. "What was so important it couldn't wait?" I asked, trying to focus on her, when all I could think about was how good Lexa had tasted on my tongue the night before.

Paige glanced nervously at the door. It was closed but not locked, and my instincts kicked in, wondering what the hell was going on. Leaning forward, she lowered her voice. "There is something weird going on in Campbell's office, Ben. This morning when I went in to grab some files, I overheard him on the phone, and he was talking to someone in Italian."

"Why is that suspicious? His daughter married some Italian guy I guess."

"He mentioned a name that my father has been following closely lately," she whispered. "Carlo Santino is a nasty bastard, from what I've heard. Some mafioso who is into human trafficking and—" She broke off when the shadow of someone walked by the door. Pressing her lips together, she waited a few seconds once they were gone to speak again. "Campbell was speaking to this guy in an agitated way, Ben. I can understand a little Italian, but I couldn't keep up with most of what I heard. But…" She blew out a frustrated breath. "But I heard your girl's name. He's up to something, and Lexa Reid is part of it."

"Fuck, Paige." Getting to my feet, I walked to the door and opened it to make sure no one was out in the hall. Seeing it was empty, I shut and locked the door before dropping down into the chair beside her. "Did anyone else hear this?"

"His secretary?" She shook her head. "I don't know. She's kind of ditzy from what I've seen. She gets his coffee like clockwork, but she knows nothing of his schedule or dealings. I'm fairly sure she's fucking him on her lunch hour though, so she might know something."

"But you're sure he was talking to Santino?" My gut felt like it was full of lead, and the thought of this bastard doing something to Lexa was making my blood boil. "The same Santino your father is looking into?"

"From the context of what I heard, my instincts are telling me yes. He's a bad man, Ben. And honestly, I'm not sure I'm comfortable continuing this investigation on my own if Campbell is working under the table with this guy. I thought when you wanted the DA looked into, you were talking about dirty politics and people paying him off to get a good deal at the most. This… My father would freak if he knew I was even in the same room with someone talking about Carlo Santino, let alone digging into his business."

I scratched at the beard growth on my chin, barely noticing the tightness in my knuckles from the stitches. "No, no. I don't want to put you in any danger either, Paige. Talk to your father. Have him get someone else to take over the investigation."

"And Lexa? What will you do about her?" Her eyes darkened with concern. "She's a target. If

Santino gets his hands on her, you probably won't ever see her again."

"I'll take care of it," I assured Paige, already making plans for how to protect my woman. "Don't worry about her."

After she left, promising me she would call her dad on her way to her new temporary apartment, I grabbed my keys. Lexa was so damn stubborn; I knew I wouldn't be able to protect her on my own. And if I didn't tell her father what Paige overheard, he would definitely kill me. Not that I would blame him.

I was using my truck until my cruiser got fixed. I'd been informed by my secretary that morning that Bash Reid was footing the bill, no doubt in hopes Campbell would go easier on his daughter. But we both knew she would be better off taking a chance on getting in front of a judge than accepting any offer Campbell tried to make. The dirty bastard wouldn't go easy on her simply because of who her father was.

The parking lot was half full when I pulled in and walked around to the garage bays. My cruiser was already in one, and Bash was standing beside it, writing down the damages on a clipboard.

"Got a minute?" I called out, grabbing his attention.

His eyes were so much like Lexa's that when he turned them on me, all I could think about for a moment was her.

Tossing the clipboard onto a huge toolbox, he walked toward me. "What do you want?" he growled, stopping a foot from me.

"We need to talk," I told him, glancing around at all the other mechanics. "It's important."

Something in my tone must have conveyed to him I wasn't joking around. Those blue eyes narrowed for a moment, before he nodded toward the shop. "Let's go to the office."

Following him inside, I saw that a teenage boy who looked a lot like Bash was behind the counter, taking care of the half-dozen customers in line. "Max, I'm going to be in the office for a bit," Bash told him. "Someone comes back this way, tell them to mind their own fucking business."

"Yes, sir," the boy said with a nod, his blue eyes narrowed on me just like his Dad's had been earlier.

In the office, Bash motioned toward the single chair sitting in front of a tidy desk as he closed the door behind him. "What's this about?"

"I assume you know who Carlo Santino is?"

His entire body seemed to jerk at the mention of that name. Opening the door, he stuck his head out. "Max!"

"Yeah, Dad?"

"You have five minutes to get everyone out of the shop. Once you do, let me know."

"Ah, come on," the boy complained. "I can barely work this damn computer. I'm not Lexa!"

"Damn right, you aren't. Now get your ass to work and get these people out of here." Slamming the door, he leaned back against it. "Don't say another word until he tells me they're all gone."

I nodded my understanding. Then I got a text from Paige, telling me she'd talked to her dad and that she needed to talk to me. I told her I would meet her for lunch and put the phone back in my pocket, waiting.

Eight minutes later, there was finally a knock on the door. "I'm done," Max said when Bash cracked it open. "You gonna kill the sheriff and didn't want witnesses?"

"Shut up, boy. Now I want you to stand outside the front door. No one comes in this building. You hear me? Not even your sister." Max's eyes widened, but he nodded. "Good. Now, go."

Holding the door open, Bash watched his son do as he was told before shutting it again. Facing me once more, he crossed his arms over his chest. "What the fuck is this about Santino?"

"First, you should know Paige, that woman I've been seen around town with? She's the special investigator into Campbell. This morning, she overheard a phone call Campbell was having. He was speaking in Italian, so she only understood part of the conversation, but from what she did hear, he was speaking to Santino."

"Dirty motherfucker," Bash groused as he walked behind the desk and took a seat. "Always knew he was in someone's pocket. Probably a lot of someones, but I never suspected it would be Santino. I should have, though."

"Paige heard him mention Lexa."

The air in the room suddenly seemed to crackle with a dangerous energy, and I was sure I'd just seen lightning flash in the man's eyes. "My little girl's name passed that fucker's lips while he was speaking to Carlo goddamn Santino?"

"That's what Paige told me," I confirmed, popping my knuckles on my uninjured hand. They ached to pound on both Campbell and Santino. Either of those bastards simply thinking of Lexa stirred the monster just below the surface. "Just hearing Campbell talk to Santino spooked Paige, so she's talking to her father about getting another investigator on the case. But I knew I needed to tell you about this. I'll focus everything on Lexa."

He nodded, which surprised the hell out of me. "I want to tell you to fuck off, but Lexa is so damn stubborn, she will throw a fit and a half if I put my own men on this. If we don't tell her and just make sure we have eyes on her at all times, we should be good." His face was gray, his jaw clenching and unclenching. "This is already a fucking nightmare. When Fontana took her, she nearly died. I can't let that happen again, Davis. I'll lose my mind."

"How bad was it?" I didn't even know if I could stomach hearing his answer, but I needed him to tell me just how close to losing her I'd come, long before I'd even gotten the chance to love her.

"When we found her, she was covered in blood, and we thought she was dead then and there. As soon as we got her to the hospital, they took her from us, and we didn't see her for hours. She had emergency surgery to repair internal bleeding from where the motherfucker had beaten her so badly, he'd ruptured internal organs. The surgeon was damn good, or that scar on her beautiful face would have been ten times worse. She was in pain for months." He ran his fingers through his dark hair that was lightly streaked with a few gray hairs at the temples. "But it wasn't just physical pain that kept her up at night. This town is full of gossiping busybodies who have nothing better to do. No one knew the real story about what happened to her, so they started making up their own versions."

"People do seem to love talking about her," I muttered. They all needed to keep their mouths shut. I was already sick and tired of everyone spooking her by talking about us.

"We're not telling her or her mother about Santino. Lexa will only try to evade us, and Raven doesn't need the extra stress right now of worrying about our baby girl," Bash said, pulling my focus back to the issue at hand. "You or your people stick to her like glue if she's not home. I'll make sure there is always someone at my house."

Keeping this from Lexa wasn't what I wanted to do, but I would take her father's lead on this. I knew just how stubborn she was, so I needed to trust his judgment for now.

Another text came in, and I glanced down at it in annoyance, expecting it to be Paige. Seeing it was Lexa, some of my tension eased just a bit, and I texted her back before lifting my gaze back to her father.

He was watching me intently, and I lifted a brow at him. "What?"

Grimacing, he shook his head. "I could tell it was Lexa just from the look on your face. Even after that night we talked about Campbell, I didn't want to believe you loved her. It was too soon. You barely knew her. You still barely know her, but I can see that you do."

"I do," I rasped out, needing him to understand just how much his daughter meant to me. "I would give up my own life to protect her.

She's everything to me. And yes, I know it hasn't been long enough by everyone else's standards, but I knew the night I first met her that she was mine."

"Then I suggest you don't fuck it up, boy."

SEVENTEEN

Hannigans' parking lot was already getting crowded that evening when I arrived.

As I walked through the bar, several of the MC brothers called out greetings to me, and I got a kiss on the cheek from both Uncle Raider and Uncle Colt, who were running the place that night.

Uncle Colt grabbed my chin as he pulled back, examining my cheek closely. "And your pops still hasn't dealt with Murphy?"

I shrugged, not sure what my dad was going to do about the deputy, and honestly, I didn't care if he did something or not. I was beyond the point of caring about anything. I'd switched something off to keep from feeling the hurt Mrs. Davis's words had caused earlier, and I wasn't ready to turn it on again any time soon.

"Rave seen this?" Uncle Raider asked, his eyes narrowed on my wrists.

"She saw it this morning. And before you ask, I'm pretty sure she's going to deal with Murphy herself. And Dad." I shrugged again. "He's on her shit list too."

The two younger Hannigan brothers shared a look before grimacing. "Well, Murphy's dead. Maybe we should send flowers," Uncle Raider muttered.

"I have work to do," I told them as I grabbed a bottle of Coke from the cooler behind the bar. I started to walk away, but I turned back at the last second. "And if the sheriff comes in looking for me, you don't know who he's talking about."

"Gotcha, sweetheart," Uncle Colt assured me with a wink. Of the four brothers, Colt and Jet looked the most alike, but Uncle Colt was the most easygoing of them all. Which didn't really mean a whole lot since he could be a hard-ass like everyone else in the Hannigan family. Still, he was easier to talk to than the others, and I loved him a little more than the other three because of it.

Walking into the back office, I got to work. Mom said the bar and Uncle Spider's place were the worst to do the books for. I understood why as soon as I sat down and saw the crumpled-up liquor supply invoice and other bills scattered across the desk. None of it was electronic like some of the other businesses Mom did the books for, like Aggie's and Barker's Construction, even though there was a perfectly good, state-of-the-art computer sitting right in the middle of the desk. Mom was the only one who used it, though, when she input the accounts into the system.

An hour into it and my head was throbbing. I was about to cry mercy when I got a text from Ben asking where I was.

Ignoring it, I grabbed the bottle of aspirin out of the top drawer of the desk and popped two before tossing my now-empty bottle of Coke in the trash. Needing to stretch my legs, I walked out to the bar in search of something else nonalcoholic to drink.

The occupants had only doubled during the hour I'd been in the office, and the people at the bar waiting to order was staggering. Both of my uncles looked out of humor as I grabbed a bottle of water out of the fridge and stepped back out of their way, taking a few minutes to watch them while sipping my drink.

"Hey, Lexa!" someone called from the back where the pool tables were. "Bring us a round of beers, honey."

I glanced at Uncle Raider, asking if he wanted me to do it.

"That would be a big help, sweetheart," he said, grabbing eight bottles of beer out of the fridge and putting them on a tray. "Tell Tiny I'll just put it on his tab."

Nodding, I grabbed the tray and walked back to the pool tables.

There was absolutely nothing tiny about Tiny. He was at least six and a half feet tall, with shoulders as wide as a bull and the not-so-pretty face of one to go with it. He and seven of his friends grabbed the bottles off the tray, and he gave me a warm smile. He might not have been fun to look at, but he'd always been kind to me.

"Uncle Raider said he'd put it on your tab," I informed him after he'd hugged me.

"Thanks, honey. Thought we were going to die of thirst back here until I saw your sweet face."

"I'm always happy to help," I said with a smile. "But I have to get back to work. Enjoy your night, fellas."

For the next two hours, I worked my way through the rest of the receipts and finally got them all logged in to the accounting program on the computer. But that was only after I'd called to whine to Mom about it and beg her to walk me through a better way of dealing with her brothers' chaos.

Shutting down the computer, I grabbed my things and exited the office.

I'd noticed the steady increase of noise out in the bar during the last hour or so, but I wasn't prepared for the almost deafening roar of the crowd when I opened the door. Everyone was having a hell of a good time. Maybe too good, from the looks of it.

Uncle Hawk was now behind the bar with his two younger brothers, but they still couldn't get the drinks out fast enough. From the pool table area, the noise was the worst, though. Drunk bikers and a group of younger guys were back there, roughhousing and arguing. It didn't take two seconds for me to realize why. My dad's cousins,

Tanner and Matt, were pool sharks, always scamming idiots who didn't know any better out of their money.

I'd never seen them in action before, though, but I'd heard plenty of stories over the years of all the money they'd won from frat boys or just about anyone who didn't know the Reid brothers and their killer skills with a pool stick.

Curious, I squeezed through the crowd, trying to get to the back without being noticed. If either of my uncles saw me watching the guys playing, they would kick me out. Especially now that the place was getting crazy and I was officially done with the books for the week.

Tiny was still standing around the same pool table he'd occupied earlier, but he and his friends were more interested in what was going on at Matt and Tanner's table than their own. Sitting on stools, they watched the entertainment, and I figured I was safest from the chaos and the view of my uncles with him.

Seeing me, Tiny grinned and draped an arm over my shoulders.

Tiny was thirty and like family. He and all his friends were since they were MC brothers. I didn't call them uncle, but they still treated me like I was a beloved niece. I leaned into him, feeling just as safe with him as I would have with my dad.

"Is it always this crazy?" I had to shout for him to hear me even as close as we were.

I felt more than heard him chuckle, his massive body shaking from the force of it. "Worse, darlin'. Those boys always stir up trouble."

Turning my gaze back to my cousins, I watched as Matt twirled his pool stick in one hand. I could barely make out him calling his shot before leaning over and sinking the ball exactly as he'd promised. Everyone behind him screamed, some with excitement, even fewer of them with disdain. The two guys they must have been hustling turned red with anger, their hands curling into fists so tightly their knuckles turned white.

Tanner sat on his stool at the other end of the table, casually drinking a bottle of beer and watching with bored eyes the same shade of blue as my own. Matt sank another ball, then ran his mouth to one of the younger guys who had pure hate shining out of his brown eyes.

I knew it was going to happen before the other guy actually moved. The pool stick in the guy's hand cracked across Matt's sternum, and he doubled over as all the air was knocked out of him. I cringed, pretty sure Matt now had some broken ribs. But before I could rush over to check on my family member, Tiny was pushing me behind him.

Bending, I watched from under his arm as Tanner laid out the guy who'd just attacked his younger brother. The second guy they'd been hustling shouted something and charged at him, but Tanner sidestepped him at the last minute, causing the guy's fist to connect with the guy behind him.

"Oh shit," I thought I heard Tiny say, and I had to blink a few times before I could believe my own eyes.

Ben stood there, not even dazed by the punch he'd just taken to the face. His jaw was tense as he grabbed the man's arm and twisted it behind him before sweeping his feet out from under him and making him drop face first to the ground.

"You're under arrest, motherfucker," he snarled, spitting on the floor at the guy's head. Only then did I realize there was blood in the spit.

He slapped cuffs on the guy's wrists, then kicked him before turning to do the same to the guy Tanner had taken down. "Anyone else?" he barked to the crowd that was now deathly silent. "No? How about you?" he shot at Tiny as he stalked forward. Ben's brandy-brown eyes caught hold of mine, and I jerked back, hiding more securely behind Tiny's massive body. "Move aside so I can get to my woman, or I'll arrest your ass, too."

I grabbed the back of Tiny's cut, holding on to it like a lifeline. "Don't do it, Tiny."

"Whatever you want, darlin'." Tiny's friends moved in around him, completely barricading me from Ben. "Don't think she considers herself your woman, Sheriff," Tiny told him. "And until she says otherwise, I'm not moving."

"Lexa," Ben growled, making me shiver because I freaking loved the sound of his voice like that. "You didn't answer any of my texts or calls all night, and I had to drive around this damn town for three hours looking for you. Then I walk in here, and you're feet away from someone getting their chest caved in with a damn pool stick? I'm about to lose my freaking mind, woman. Get your ass out here so I can check for myself that you're okay."

"No thanks. I'm good right here."

"Lexa." His voice was thick with warning, which I ignored. After what had happened with his grandmother, I wasn't going to give in.

My mom was the one person in the world who knew me the best. I had to assume that his grandmother probably did, in fact, know Ben better than anyone too. She would know if he was only playing with me before getting back together with Paige. Which was exactly what I'd been afraid of all along. I wasn't going to give in, not even with that sexy-as-hell tone of voice he was using on me.

I needed to have at least a little self-respect.

"What the fuck is going on in here?"

I jerked at the rage-filled sound of my father's voice, and Tiny stood up a little straighter. From under his arm, I spotted Dad, Uncle Spider, and Uncle Jet. They walked through the parting crowd like biker gods in their aged leather cuts, while people looked on with total and complete awe at the deities they were.

A groan alerted me to Matt again, and he stood up, his cough a horrible sound as he rubbed at his chest. "Fucking pussies couldn't take a little heckling. Broke his pool stick on me."

"Tanner, take him to the hospital."

Matt groaned. "Damn it, Bash. Rory is going to kick my ass if I call her from the emergency room again."

Dad didn't even blink at his younger cousin. "Then maybe you shouldn't end up there so much."

"Truth," Tanner said with a laugh as he pulled his brother's arm over his shoulder. "I need a car."

"Lexa," Dad called out. "Give Tanner your keys."

Sighing heavily, I nudged Tiny, and he stepped aside, letting me pass. I gave Tanner my keys, then started to walk past Ben to my dad.

His hand grasped my wrist before I could make it an inch by him. "I'll give you a ride home, baby."

I tried to jerk out of his hold, but his grip only tightened. Not painfully but enough to let me know he wasn't going to let go anytime soon, so I needed to give in. I glanced at my dad for help. "Dad—"

"Davis is going to take you home, Lexa," he informed me with that same hard bite to his voice. "Don't give him any lip."

"But—"

"What about these two?" Dad asked Ben, speaking over any protest I would have voiced.

"I'll have one of my deputies pick them up and book them. That one is getting the full treatment for assault on an officer." Ben tucked me against him, his other hand stroking down my spine. "Any paperwork I need to file can be done in the morning, though. I'll be at your house."

Dad only nodded as Ben walked me out of the bar, and I couldn't keep my mouth from gaping a little at the bizarreness of the whole incident, thinking maybe I'd stepped into some weird twilight zone or something.

EIGHTEEN

BEN

Lexa's silence was worse than nails on a chalkboard for me as I drove toward her house. With each mile that she continued to ignore me, my hands tightened a little more around the steering wheel until the stitches began to protest and blood leaked around them.

Gritting my teeth, I forced myself to relax my grip. "Is that the type of date you're used to?" Turning my gaze from the road, I glanced at her, but she continued to glare out the passenger window. "That guy, what's his name…Tiny? You like him?"

Again, no answer, and it only spiked my blood pressure higher.

"Lexa, you are killing me right now," I told her. "Why are you pissed at me? I'm the one who found you out with that Tiny asshole."

"Tiny's a good guy," she said without looking at me. "And if you must know, I wasn't out with him. The reason I was even at the bar was because I was doing the books for my mom."

"Then what's going on? What did I do now to make you mad?" Because I was coming up with nothing, no matter how hard I racked my brain for an answer. Sure, she still could have been upset about hearing Paige on the phone with me earlier, but I thought she'd gotten over it after the texts I'd gotten earlier from her thanking me for the T-shirt I'd left in her car when I'd dropped it off that morning.

Her shoulders shifted, and she finally turned her head in my direction, but the expression on her face was cold, emotionless, and I almost preferred when she was glaring out the window. "Tell me something, Ben. Are you and your grandmother close?"

Unsure where this was going, I shrugged. "Yeah, I mean, sure. She and my grandfather are all the family I have left. The three of us are pretty tight."

"And would you say she knows you better than anyone else?"

"She's my grandmother, Lexa, of course she knows me—"

But she cut me off just as I was pulling up in front of her house. "Yeah, I thought so. That's all I needed to know." Opening the door, she jumped out. "Thanks for the ride, Sheriff."

The door slammed before I'd even gotten my seat belt off. She ran up the driveway to the front door, and I took off after her. Something was going on. The look on her face as she'd glanced back at me before shutting the door had nearly broken me, and I didn't understand what had put that kind of sadness in her beautiful eyes.

But I'd fucking find out.

The front door was about to close when I grabbed it and pushed it open enough to enter the house. There were tears in her eyes, and I nearly fell to my knees then and there to plead with her to tell me what was wrong.

Instead, I cupped her face, wiping away the tears with my thumbs. "Baby, talk to me. What happened that made you cry? If I said something wrong, tell me. If someone hurt you, I'll take care of them. Just please, don't cry."

"You're right," she murmured, stepping back so that I was no longer touching her. "You're not worth my tears. Not you, and not your grandmother." She started up the stairs. "You did your job. I'm home. Now get the hell out of my house."

"Goddamn it, Lexa!" I exploded, feeling like she was really walking away for good, and that made me panic. "What the hell did I miss this time?"

"Maybe you should ask your grandmother," a new voice suggested from behind me.

Reluctantly, I looked away from Lexa's retreating back to face the woman who'd just spoken. Willa Masterson stood in the living room, two glasses of what looked like iced tea in her hands. Offering one to Felicity Hannigan, who was seated on the couch, Willa put her free hand on her hip and glared at me, while the other woman watched me with wide eyes.

"What does she have to do with any of this?" I demanded, exasperated.

"Like I said, ask her." Taking a sip of her drink, she sat down beside the other woman, crossing her legs. "Bitch was lucky I didn't scalp her on the spot," she muttered to herself as she got comfortable.

"I'm asking you," I said, moving into the living room so I could face them both.

Willa grinned, but it was the kind of grin that probably would have scared the hell out of a lesser person. "He thinks he can intimidate me, Flick."

She laughed. "Yeah, you can tell he hasn't been around long if he thinks that is possible with any female in this family." Sipping her drink, Felicity smirked up at me. "I suggest you go talk to the dear, sweet Mrs. Davis. And while you're there, tell her the Angel's Halo ol' ladies would love to have a sit-down with her whenever she gets the chance."

"Fuck," I muttered under my breath. "I can't leave Lexa."

Willa snorted. "Excuse you? She's not alone. She's got us and her mom right upstairs. Trust me on this, Sheriff. You're going to want to talk to that old hag tonight."

There was no way in hell I was leaving with just three women to protect what was mine. Pulling out my phone, I hit my grandmother's number, staring Willa down as I waited for an answer.

It rang half a dozen times, which was unlike her to let it ring for so long before answering. "Um, hi, sweetheart. How...how was your day?"

The hesitancy in her voice had my eyes narrowing. "What did you do?" I demanded, immediately knowing she had, in fact, done something. And whatever it was, that was why Lexa was so upset with me.

"Are you hungry? I got all those deli meats I know you love so much. You could come over and have a sandwich... Or I'll pack you some and bring them by the station tomorrow. We could have lunch together."

"Gran," I snapped, cutting her off before she could go on and on about damned deli meats. "I asked you a question. Answer it."

I heard her exhale heavily. "I'm so sorry, Ben. I was in the grocery store this morning, and I was gossiping with Denise Hallbeck. You know how she is, always amping me up about you. She was talking about how that Lexa Reid girl was chasing after you and how she took a baseball bat to your cruiser yesterday... And... And..."

"And what?" I bit out, feeling my blood turn cold.

"And I said you were only playing with Lexa until you finally gave Paige another chance. I-I knew I was just blowing smoke, but Denise looked so condescending, and I couldn't stand it. Well, I didn't know Lexa was standing right behind us in line at the deli."

"That's why she asked if you knew me so well," I muttered to myself. "I confirmed you knew me better than anyone, and she automatically thought you were right."

"I really am sorry." Gran sounded older all of a sudden, fragile. But that didn't stop me from being pissed off at her.

"I'll talk to you about this later. Right now, I have to go fix this mess you made."

At least, I hoped I could. The way Lexa had acted earlier, I wasn't so sure I could this time.

I ended the call even as Gran was apologizing again. Felicity and Willa looked up at me with raised brows, waiting expectantly.

"Told you that you would want to ask her," Willa groused.

"Yeah, you fucking told me," I agreed. "Now maybe you can tell me how to fix this."

Both women laughed. "Oh, honey, you think you can play games with our girl and stomp all over her heart, and when she finally—fucking finally—sees the light, that you could just snap your fingers and fix this shit?" Felicity shook her head, amusement shining out of her pansy-blue eyes.

"Yes!" I snapped at her. "Because I haven't been playing any games. I love Lexa. It's everyone else in this goddamn town who has been fucking with her head."

"Maybe you do love her. Maybe you don't," Willa said with a twist of her lips. "But right now, Lexa isn't so sure. Have you even told her how you feel, dumbass? Perhaps everyone was able to fuck with her head, as you put it, because you haven't been clear enough about this supposed love you have for her."

Fuck, she was right about that too. I hadn't told Lexa I loved her yet. No damn wonder she so easily believed all the bullshit everyone—including my own grandmother—said about me.

As I was agonizing over that fact, the doorbell rang.

Felicity got to her feet, that same smug grin on her face again. "Oh my, who could that be, I wonder," she singsonged as she walked to the door, humming happily to herself.

I was on edge even before she opened the damn thing, knowing I wasn't going to like this one little bit.

"Theo!" she exclaimed, louder than necessary for my benefit, and I balled my hands into fists as she hugged the guy standing before her. "Sweetheart, what a perfect, wonderful surprise."

"How are you, Mrs. Hannigan?" he greeted with respect and a smile I knew would melt any pussy. "Sorry to drop by without calling."

"No, no, honey, we're used to you boys popping in unexpectedly," she laughed, waving him in. "We were just talking to Sheriff Davis, who was about to leave."

"I'm not leaving." And to prove my point, I dropped down into the recliner perpendicular to the couch and met Theo's gaze head on. His dark brows lifted, a mixture of emotions in them that I couldn't clearly read, which was new for me. I put his age at about twenty, but he easily could have been either younger or older. He was a good-looking asshole, and I didn't doubt he got into girls' pants quickly enough. But what I really wanted to know was if he'd gotten into Lexa's in any way. "Especially if he's staying."

She shrugged. "We have plenty of extra rooms. Theo, you can stay in the same one as last time. It's right across the hall from Lexa's. You go on and freshen up and let Lexa know you're here."

I jumped up just as quickly as I'd sat. "The fuck, woman?" I glared at her as I stomped up the stairs after Theo to the sound of Willa laughing her ass off.

Theo didn't even glance back at me as he made his way to the room straight across from Lexa's. I stood outside her door as he opened his own. As the door closed, he gave me a cocky smirk, and I flipped him off.

As soon as the door shut, I was knocking on Lexa's. "Baby, open up," I called out, but I got no answer. Muttering a curse, I twisted the knob and stepped inside.

The room was in total darkness, and I knew before I even turned on the light that she wasn't there.

"Lexa!"

NINETEEN

I stopped outside my bedroom door, but I hesitated before opening it. My heart was hurting so damn bad, and all I really wanted was my mom.

Moving on down the hall, I knocked on my parents' door before cracking it open. I heard the TV and expected Mom to be in bed, the covers tucked in around her, relaxing. But she wasn't there. I heard a curse and looked straight at the window.

Mom was half in, half out of it, her eyes wide like a deer caught in the headlights of an oncoming eighteen-wheeler. "Well, don't just stand there, honey. Either come with me, or cover for me with your aunts."

The choice was easy enough for me. For one, I didn't know where she was going, but I knew she was going to be breaking all kinds of the doctor's rules. For another, Ben was downstairs, and I didn't know if I could face him again after he'd basically confessed his grandmother was right.

I shut and locked Mom's door then sprinted across the room. She finished climbing out, and I was right behind her.

It was easier for me to get off the roof first and then help her down. Once we were both on the ground, she took my hand and, with a wicked grin, tugged me toward the driveway. We ran two blocks before she stopped beside a parked truck I didn't recognize.

"Where are we going?" I whispered, glancing around to make sure no one was watching us as she pulled a key fob out of her pocket and unlocked the doors with the press of a button.

She tossed me the fob. "You drive. I'm still not supposed to."

Brows lifted at her, I got behind the wheel. "Really, Mom? You just ran like we were being chased by the devil himself. Pretty sure you're not supposed to do that either."

"I'm attempting to be good," she said with a snicker.

I started the truck, but I had no clue where to go. "Any particular destination in mind? Or am I going to drive aimlessly?"

She plugged an address into the GPS and sat back. "There you go."

Sighing, I started following the directions. "Where did you get this truck?"

"A friend of mine left it there for me," she said evasively.

"A friend," I repeated, unable to keep the skepticism out of my voice.

"Yes, a friend. Don't sound so surprised."

"Mom, I know every single friend you have, and none of them would have left a truck for you to sneak out in. Not right now when they know you've just had surgery."

"Lexa, by now, you should know I have friends, and then I have *friends*. Big difference, baby girl. Trust me." With a wink, she turned on the radio and scanned through the channels until she found a classic rock station.

Shaking my head at her, I focused on driving, fighting a grin.

It wasn't until I was pulling up in front of an older, one-story house that I even guessed where we were. The police car in the driveway gave it away.

"Shit, Mom," I groaned. "This is Murphy's house, isn't it?"

"Of course it is. Drive down the block a bit. We'll walk back through those trees over there."

Not for the first time, I blew out a heavy sigh, but I did as instructed. I drove several houses down, and then we sat for a few minutes, making sure no one drove or walked by before getting out. Mom led the way into the bank of trees that went along the backs of the row of houses, using her phone to see by.

Sticking close to her, I debated calling Dad to snitch on her, but I quickly vetoed that option. Whatever Mom was going to do, she would do it whether my dad made threats or not. And I honestly couldn't handle the backlash of her being upset with me even if I did call him.

Plus, I kind of wanted Murphy to get whatever punishment Mom dished out.

When we reached the one-story house again, I realized there was a six-foot privacy fence encasing the backyard.

"Give me a boost," Mom whispered.

I helped her so she could see over the fence, and for a few minutes, she scanned the yard before telling me to lift her a little higher so she could climb over. Once she was on the other side, I jumped up and over it. My height came in handy on some occasions, it seemed.

My landing was anything but perfect, but Mom caught my arm, steadying me. When I started to thank her, she put her finger to her lips, indicating for me to keep quiet, then nodded toward the back porch.

Nodding, I fixed my shirt and followed her as she stealthily moved to the rear door. It was a sliding French door that led into the kitchen, and of course, it was locked. That didn't hinder Mom any, though. She pulled something from her pocket, and I watched with my mouth gaping open while she picked the lock.

Two minutes later, the door slid open silently, and we entered the house.

The sound of male laughter alerted us to where Murphy was, but it also gave me pause. He wasn't alone. At least one other man was with him, from what I could tell. Mom and I locked gazes, and she shrugged, letting me know she had no idea who else was there.

"Santino's men will be here tonight," a voice I only vaguely recognized said through his amusement. "They'll take the whole house by surprise and get the girl. I told him not to leave a single one of them alive."

The laughter came again before Murphy spoke. "What's he planning on doing with the girl?"

"Why?" the other man jeered. "You want a turn with her before he gets his hands on her?"

"Damn, man, have you seen her? That body is perfect even if the scar turns my stomach."

I froze in place, realizing he had to be talking about me. That could only mean they were talking about this Santino guy breaking in to my house and killing my family.

Mom reached back, her fingers cold as they clutched at mine. But even as she locked her hand around mine, I saw the gun she pulled from a holster strapped to her ankle.

"Of course I want to have a turn. See what all the fuss is about since fucking Davis can't stop freaking out over the bitch," Murphy continued.

"Wouldn't mind a round or two with her myself," the other guy told him.

My stomach turned as they so casually talked about raping me like I was nothing more than a sex doll they wanted to put their dicks in. I felt Mom starting to shake, and I knew her rage was about to cause complete mayhem.

Knowing I couldn't let her do it without a weapon of my own, I glanced around the kitchen. Spotting the knife block, I grabbed the biggest handle, earning me an approving nod from Mom.

"Stay behind me," she mouthed, and because she had the gun, I reluctantly agreed.

The men were still talking about how they both wanted to fuck me—rape me, because there was no way in hell I would ever let either of them touch me willingly. Mom released my hand and got down on all fours, crawling into the living room. Of course, I followed behind her, crawling as stealthily as possible considering I was a freaking giant.

Murphy and his guest, who I recognized as Royce Campbell as soon as I saw the side of his face, were sitting on the couch. Knowing it was the dirty DA who was talking about me only made me want to puke.

Using sign language—something she'd taught both Max and me when we were younger so we could communicate when speaking wasn't possible—Mom told me she was going to put the gun to Campbell's head, then instructed me to either slit Murphy's throat or put the knife to it. I was going with the latter for the moment.

Lifting her hand, she counted down from three, and then everything felt like it was moving in slow motion. She jumped up, putting the gun right at Campbell's temple. Before Murphy could even react, I grabbed his hair in one hand and had the butcher knife pressed flush against his throat with the other. If he so much as swallowed hard, he would get a smooth shave.

"What the fuck is this?" Campbell bellowed, yet he didn't move. "How did you two get in here?"

"I have my ways," Mom said, her voice sounding bored even though I could see the fire burning in her green eyes. "I only came to show my respect for Murphy here and got a bonus in the process."

"You—" He didn't get to finish whatever he was saying because she moved the gun from his temple to his mouth, shoving it in, making him whine in pain when I heard a few teeth actually crack.

"I'll do the talking, motherfucker," she seethed before turning her gaze on Murphy. "Hi, Deputy. How the hell have you been?"

"Mrs. R-Reid," he stuttered.

"Now, you tell me, Murphy. Was it really necessary to treat my daughter so roughly last night? You left physical proof you weren't playing fair." She shook her head in disappointment. "I wouldn't even be here if you had arrested her without bruising her. But that scrape on her cheek, man, that's going to cost you even more."

"I-I'm sorry, Mrs. Reid. Really...I was... I was only doing my job, ma'am. She put up a...a fight. I had..." He swallowed roughly, and the sound of the blade of my knife scraping over his throat filled the room. "Please don't kill me."

She laughed, the sound making the deputy actually tremble and goose bumps to rise on my arms. "I won't kill you if you tell me everything Santino has planned. Deal?" He tried to nod, but my blade didn't give him much room. "Good boy."

The laugh stopped cold when she looked back at Campbell. "You, on the other hand… Oh, I'm going to kill you. And Murphy's going to help me do it. That way, *if* he walks away from this, he can't rat me out without telling on himself in the process."

***

There was blood on my shirt that wasn't my own. It had a strong metallic scent to it that made me want to gag, but I stopped myself before I could every time.

Murphy stood over Campbell's dead body, his face covered in more blood splatter than my shirt. With the knife I'd brought from the kitchen, he'd slit his boss's throat while Mom held a gun pointed

229

at his heart. He hadn't even flinched as he'd done it, but Campbell had begged like the pussy he was.

"Now," Mom said as she stood over the DA's lifeless body, the gun still pointed unwaveringly at the deputy. "About Santino."

Face white as death, Murphy started talking in a voice several octaves higher than normal in his anxiety. "They're supposed to hit your house at two o'clock. I don't know how many will be with them, but I know they are planning to take your daughter and then kill the rest of you. Santino wants Lexa for himself before he sells her."

"Sells me?" I repeated, equal parts pissed and scared of what could have happened if we hadn't gotten a heads-up like this.

"Santino's into human trafficking," Mom informed me. "He's probably the top dealer right now."

A shudder went down my spine, and I seriously couldn't stop the images that filled my head.

"He's not going to touch you," she vowed when she noticed my reaction. "I can promise you that, sweetheart."

Headlights flashed through the living room window as a vehicle pulled into the driveway, followed by two more. Mom muttered a curse and quickly put the gun back in her ankle holster before walking casually to the front door just as a pounding fist knocked.

"Raven!" Dad shouted.

Murphy seemed to cower even more at the sound of my dad's voice, but that was nothing compared to his reaction to Ben when he pushed through my dad and two of my uncles. Murphy seemed to shrink, trying to make himself as small as possible.

"Lexa," Ben breathed my name when he saw me, his face relaxing somewhat. "Are you hurt?"

Before I could even answer, he was in front of me, his hands skimming over me to check for injuries. When he touched the still-wet blood on my shirt, his brown eyes became black in a heartbeat. "Are. You. Hurt?" he gritted out.

"No, of course not," I rushed to assure him.

"Then whose blood is this?"

"Not mine," I said evasively, trying to pretend like I wasn't enjoying every second of his hands on me. Why did my damn body have to betray me and melt for him every time he was this close? It wasn't fair.

That was when he took in the rest of the room and finally noticed the dead man lying on Murphy's floor. "What the fuck happened here?" he raged.

"What do you think happened, Sheriff?" Mom countered with a question of her own.

Ben's eyes went from Campbell to her, to Murphy and the knife lying at his feet where he'd dropped it. Ben took it all in within a matter of seconds before answering her. "It looks like you two paid Murphy a friendly visit, but Campbell interrupted and tried to ambush you to take Lexa. Murphy had no choice but to defend you with the only weapon on hand."

Mom's grin was bright enough to light up the whole world. "Smart man. That's exactly what happened. Right, Murphy?"

"Y-Yes, ma'am," he whispered, his voice trembling just as much as his body was.

Dad, Uncle Spider, Uncle Jet, and Uncle Hawk were all in the living room with us now, making the small space feel almost claustrophobic.

"Bash, I have to tell you about Santino," Mom told him. "He's planning a hit on the house tonight. We need to get Lexa to a safe house until we get this bastard taken care of. I don't know why he's suddenly got his sights set on her, but he does."

"I've got it covered, baby," Dad told her, but instead of soothing Mom, that only made her take several steps away from him.

"What do you mean, you have it covered? I only just told you…" She narrowed her eyes. "You knew already. You fucking knew, and you didn't tell me our daughter was in danger?"

"I can explain," he started, but she backed away from him until she was standing only inches from me. "Raven—"

"Don't Raven me!" she screamed at him. "You don't get to play God with our child's life. I'm sick, not dead, you dickhead. If something is going on with one of our kids, I have the right to know."

"I didn't want you to worry. The doctor said for you to take things easy. Fuck, babe, you snuck out to come to Murphy's house, and look what the hell happened. Davis and I had it under control."

It was my turn to narrow my eyes. Ben met my gaze, but I didn't see a single ounce of remorse in his eyes. He was going to keep the fact that I was on some sadist's list from me? Fuck, I didn't think he could hurt me more than he already had, but I was wrong. I always seemed to be when it came to him.

"I have a suggestion." A voice I recognized immediately, yet couldn't believe was actually there, spoke up for the first time, and I turned my head to find Theo leaning in the open doorway.

"Theo!" I cried and jerked away from Ben and pushed past two of my uncles to get to him, wrapping my arms around his waist. "What are you doing here?"

"Something told me I should check in on you. Your texts said one thing, but I got the feeling they meant something else." He hugged me back, kissing the top of my head.

"You have a suggestion?" Uncle Jet reminded him.

"Yeah. The Vitucci jet is at my disposal. It's at the airport right now waiting on me since I only planned to stay a day or two. I can take Lexa back to New York with me—"

"No fucking way," Ben growled from right behind me, but I refused to even look at him.

"—until you get the Santino thing dealt with," he continued as if he hadn't been interrupted. "She can either stay with my parents or with Cristiano and Anya. There's no way Santino could touch her there."

"He's right," Uncle Jet confirmed. "Cristiano will ensure she's safe, and we wouldn't have to worry about her while we deal with this."

"It's Lexa's choice," Dad said after a tense moment. "If she wants to, she can go. If she doesn't, we have safe houses she can stay in."

I was surprised he was even giving me a choice, but it wasn't me he was looking at when he made the offer. He was doing it in an attempt to soothe Mom, but she didn't seem to be appeased. It was going to take a lot to get him out of the doghouse this time.

Ben's hands were heavy when they landed on my shoulders, forcibly turning me to face him and pulling me away from Theo. His eyes were back to that same brandy-brown I loved so much as they implored me. "Stay here," he commanded in a hoarse voice. "I'll protect you, I swear it. Santino won't dare to touch you. But, please, just stay."

TWENTY

Holding my breath, I waited for Lexa's answer. If she went with Theo, I knew in my gut, I would never see her again.

That thought alone made me break out in a cold sweat.

Stepping back, she forced me to release her yet again. "Did you mean it, Dad?" she asked Bash. "Do I really have a choice in this?"

"I mean it."

She closed her eyes and blew out a heavy exhale. "Then I choose neither," she told him. "I'm not going anywhere."

"Lexa—" Bash started.

"Lexa, you have to," Raven spoke over him. "Honey, Santino doesn't bluff. He will come after you."

She shrugged. "I'll take my chances, but I'm not leaving you. You start chemo soon, and I'm going to be right here with you while you go through it."

"I would feel better knowing you were safely away from that bastard's grasp."

"He said I have a choice. This is what I'm choosing," Lexa stubbornly informed her mom. "I'm not going anywhere."

"Let's get her moved to the clubhouse," Bash instructed Masterson. "Her, Raven, and Flick. Now."

"On it," the enforcer said with a nod.

"Felicity will pack them each a bag," Jet said as he texted rapidly.

Her choice didn't make me feel smug. She wasn't staying for me, but fuck, it was a relief just to have her agreeing to stay at all.

"What do you need me to do?" Theo asked, still standing in the doorway.

"I'll let you know," Bash said.

My gaze went back to Campbell's lifeless body lying on the floor, the blood pooled around him from the gaping slash across his throat. I didn't know how the two Reid women had gotten Murphy to kill the DA, and I wasn't about to ask. The less I knew of the truth, the better.

Murphy himself looked like he was about to vomit or pass out, maybe both. I didn't know if it was because this was his first kill, or if he was just so scared right then, his body couldn't take it. Either way, the pussy needed to man up.

"I have to deal with this, and then I'll meet you at your clubhouse," I told Bash, reluctantly agreeing to let him take Lexa with him.

I could get a statement from her and Raven later. For now, I needed to call the coroner and get Murphy dealt with too.

"I'll let the men at the gate know you're coming," Bash said as he motioned for Raven and Lexa to leave.

Raven flipped him off as she passed him, then put her arm around Lexa's shoulders and walked with her out to the SUV Bash drove. I'd called him when I realized neither Lexa nor her mom was in the house, and he'd nearly burst my eardrum when he'd started yelling and cursing. He told me where they would probably be, and somehow, we'd gotten there at the same time even though he'd been farther away at the Hannigans' bar.

As the house slowly emptied of people, I pulled out my phone and called in the dead body, already thinking of how I was going to explain this so it would seem like a legit self-defense kill. I knew I could come up with a story that would fit everything. The problem was, would Murphy corroborate it?

"Are you going to be sick?" I asked him.

He shook his head, but no sooner had he'd confirmed he wasn't, than he bent over, puking right into the puddle of blood at his feet. But vomiting wasn't his only problem. He began to shake, and I caught him under the shoulders just as his legs finally gave out and he passed out cold.

Laying him down on the floor away from Campbell, I felt for a pulse, making sure he was okay. Vaguely, I remembered overhearing he had a heart condition. When I didn't feel a pulse, I cursed and started doing CPR.

"Need a hand?"

I looked up, surprised anyone was left in the house, especially him. Theo crouched down beside me, nodding to the deputy I was trying to save.

"What are you still doing here?" I demanded.

"You're my ride. I rode here with you, and since there was no room for me in the other vehicles, figured I needed to leave the way I came." Shrugging, he didn't seem all that concerned for the dying man beneath my hands. "Want me to call an ambulance, or take over compressions while you do it?"

Gritting my teeth, I let him take over while I called for an ambulance.

***

I didn't get to the clubhouse until over an hour later. Between having to deal with Murphy, who'd died on scene at his house, and the coroner, I was fed up with everything by the time I walked in with Theo at my side.

If I weren't so damn jealous of the asshole wanting Lexa, I might have actually liked him. He'd kept his cool during the whole situation with my now-dead deputy and tried his hardest to keep him alive until the paramedics showed up to take over. But whatever heart condition Murphy had, the stress of the evening had finished him, and not even defibrillating him repeatedly could restart his heart.

As we walked inside, Bash called down from the second floor, waving me up to what must have been his office. I hesitated, looking around for Lexa, needing to see her if only for just a second before this night got any crazier. But she wasn't anywhere in sight, and I knew I didn't have time to go looking for her.

Theo was already halfway up the stairs before I even moved in that direction. Popping my neck to ease some of the tension building in my muscles, I took the stairs two at a time and walked into the office. Over a dozen MC brothers were already there, and Bash motioned for me to shut the door before speaking.

"We all know Sheriff Davis," he introduced. "And Adrian Volkov's son, Theo, will also be sitting in on this."

Theo got nods, while I got a few glares. It didn't bother me any. I wasn't there to be their friend. I was there to do whatever the fuck I could to help keep Lexa safe.

"Santino will be hitting my house at two," Bash told them. "From what Raven got out of Murphy, that's basically all we know."

"What's your plan?" Jet was the one to ask.

"The women stay here. I've already called Matt to make sure Rory and Chance come here so they aren't in the line of fire..." He gave us the rundown of the plan, and I was quick to agree with it.

"We need to move now if we want to be in place in time," Hawk told him. "Otherwise, they might change their plans."

"Agreed," Bash said. "I only want enough men who will fit in my SUV. We'll pull into the garage so no one can see who does or doesn't get out, because I know those fuckers are watching the house."

"I'm going," I volunteered.

"You sure about that?" he asked with lifted brows. "You're stirring up a lot of attention tonight, Sheriff. People are going to talk tomorrow about how you're helping us out."

"I don't give a fuck what people say."

"Yeah, but maybe we do," Jet said, giving me a strange look. "This attention could be bad for you when it comes to the election, and maybe—just maybe—we like having you as the sheriff around here."

"Two weeks ago, my being the sheriff was keeping me from Lexa. What changed?" I demanded. I would give up my position in a heartbeat if that was what it took to be with her. Now they wanted me to stay sheriff?

Bash shrugged his wide shoulders. "Maybe we trust you…just a little bit." He rolled his eyes. "Don't let that go to your head, though."

A smirk teased at my lips. "Wouldn't think of it."

"And maybe Bash here was thinking you would be his son-in-law eventually," Jet jeered. "And he figures having the sheriff in the family would make life a little easier around here for us."

"Yeah, maybe," Bash said with another shrug.

"Are you telling me I can't go, then?" I asked.

"Let's just say it's better for everyone involved if the law didn't see us cleaning up the mess we're about to make."

"But Volkov is going?" I found myself growling, not liking one damn bit that they were taking the other guy.

"Theo is just as good a shot as our sniper. Fuck yeah, he's going." Jet smacked Theo on the back. "Plus, Vitucci would throw a fit if we take out some of Santino's men and his nephew wasn't there to share in the fun."

"Yeah, yeah, just don't let my mom find out about this," Theo grumbled. "I don't need that kind of drama right now, man."

I popped my neck again. I wanted to go, but I understood their reasons for wanting me to stay as far away from what was about to happen as possible. I needed to be able to cover for them if something happened and everything went south. And if I were caught in the middle of that shit, I wouldn't have the credibility to keep them out of trouble.

"Keep your phone close," Bash told me in a low voice as the others started filing out of the office. "Stay on standby in case we need backup after all."

Jaw clenched, I nodded.

"She's in her room. Third door on the left once you go through the main room downstairs. Whatever is going on between you two, sort it out and fast. I don't like seeing my baby girl like this." He slapped me on the shoulder as he followed his men, and I watched them go until they were out the front door before going in search of my woman.

TWENTY-ONE

 LEXA

My room at the clubhouse compound was one I'd used off and on during my childhood. After getting the scar, those times had been few and far between, but this was bringing back all kinds of upsetting memories.

No one had to stress how bad Santino being interested in me was. It was his man who'd given me the consolation prize I saw every time I looked in the mirror after all. A man like that had to work for someone who was ten times as bad.

But I wasn't going to run and hide like the scared little girl they'd made me. I had a life to live, and a mom who needed me here with her—no matter how many times she begged me to go to one of the safe houses. Or better yet, go to New York and hide behind Ciro Donati and Cristiano Vitucci.

Yeah, that wasn't going to happen.

Scared I might be, but a coward I was not.

A tap on the door had me blinking into the darkened room. There were no windows, and the door was the only point of entry, so no one could sneak up on me. I'd locked it because I wanted to be left alone, but any one of the MC brothers could easily pick the lock if they had to.

"No, I'm not hungry," I called out, figuring it was one of the sheep come to baby me. "Or thirsty. Yes. I have plenty of pillows, clean sheets, and a fresh comforter. Go away."

The knock came again, and I groaned as I climbed out of bed and stomped across the room to jerk the door open.

My eyes barely had time to adjust to the light from the hall before Ben was cupping the back of my head with one hand, wrapping his other arm around me to anchor me against his hard body. His mouth crashed down on mine in a kiss that stole my breath.

Walking me backward without breaking the kiss or putting so much as an inch between our bodies, he closed the door and flipped the lock before picking me up and carrying me the rest of the way to the bed.

I didn't have time to think, and even if I did, I probably wouldn't have. All I wanted was to feel. His hands, his lips, his body pressing me into the mattress. I could barely breathe from how hard he was kissing me, like he would die if he stopped even for a second, but I loved it.

My shirt and bra disappeared before I even realized he was pulling them off me. When I felt his fingers working on the snap and zipper of my jeans, I arched my hips up enough for him to push them and my panties down my legs. Cool air hit my drenched sex, and I gasped into his mouth, goose bumps popping up along my entire body.

"I need light," he muttered, pulling back and trying to see through the dark. "I want to look at you."

"No," I whined, pulling his head back down for another kiss. "It will take too long. I need you now."

Tugging his work shirt out of his pants, I tore at the buttons, wanting to feel the skin underneath. His body was hot to the touch and rock hard. I stroked my fingertips up and down his abs, delighting in the defined edges of his six-pack before attacking his belt buckle.

When my hand dipped into his pants and boxers, wrapping around his girth, we both groaned. The tip was already sticky with proof of how much he wanted me, and I massaged it into his flesh, using it to lube his shaft as I stroked him from tip to base and back again.

"You're killing me," he whispered beside my ear just before his teeth sank into the tender skin of my neck. "Are you ready for me, beautiful?"

"Yes," I moaned. "Please, Ben."

Kicking his pants and boxer briefs the rest of the way off, he used his knees to part my thighs and sank into me. We both held our breath as he pushed past the proof of my virginity, and then he was all the way inside me.

I felt stretched to capacity, tender, and ultrasensitive to every breath he took while he gave my body a moment to adjust to his delicious invasion.

"You okay?" he asked. "Want me to stop?"

"At this point, I think stopping would kill us both," I murmured, shifting my hips to test how sore I was. When all I felt was a slight burn that quickly turned into pleasure, I relaxed, and he was able to go a little deeper than he already was.

"Fuck, you feel good," he growled, his hands gripping my ass hard. "I don't ever want to move from this spot for the rest of my life."

Sweat was already coating both our bodies. I scratched my nails down his back, making him shudder in pleasure, his cock jerking inside my tightness. "Wish I could let you, but I'm about to lose my mind if you don't make me come, Ben."

He pulled out, just a little, and slammed back in. Stars flashed before my eyes, and I clenched them shut as I lifted my hips to meet his next thrust. His cock hit something deep inside that had a little mewling sound leaving my throat. I kissed his chest, the only part of him my lips could reach right then. He tasted like sweat and something tangier.

I was already right on the edge, and his slow, steady pace was only making me hungrier. "Harder," I begged shamelessly. "Please, harder."

His fingers flexed on my ass, and he ground down into me. I whimpered in pleasure, my nails breaking through the skin on his upper back and slicing as I tried to hold on to the moment. I wanted to come, yet it felt so good, I wanted it to last too. But then he pulled almost completely out and slammed back in, thrusting so hard the bed frame knocked against the wall. My sex clamped down around him so firmly, he started cursing.

Seconds later, I was crying his name just as he shouted mine…

An indeterminate amount of time later, the sweat had cooled on our bodies, but we were still connected in the most intimate of ways. I could feel how hard he still was and couldn't help wondering if he was always like that, or if he was debating going for round two. I wasn't opposed to another orgasm, but I was exhausted and sleep was already making my lashes feel like they had ten-pound weights tied to them.

The same thing happened the night before when he snuck in to my bedroom at home. No sooner had he gotten me off than I passed out. I just didn't know if I liked that he could so easily knock me out. An orgasm or two and then I was a puddle of goo for him to do with whatever he wanted.

Turning us on our sides, he pillowed my head on one arm and used the other to hold me against his body. His fingers stroking little circles on my hip did nothing to help me fight the urge to fall asleep in his arms.

"Hey." His voice was soft, imploring as he lifted my chin and made me look at him. Not that I could make out more than the shape of his face with the lights off, but I could picture the intense expression on it. "There's something important I need to tell you."

Every muscle in my body tensed, and the sleepiness completely evaporated as I prepared for him to tell me this really was all a game and now that he'd gotten off, he wanted to be with Paige after all.

"I love you," he murmured, his lips brushing over mine so softly, tears stung my eyes.

"Wait, what?" I whispered, not sure I'd heard him correctly. Maybe I was already asleep, and this was just a dream.

"I love you, beautiful." Another brush to my lips as he thrust into me and held himself deep.

Swallowing the knot of emotion trying to choke me, I sucked in a deep breath, savoring this moment. "Ben—"

"Shh," he commanded, suddenly sitting up in bed.

"Why?" I looked around, straining my ears to listen for whatever he'd just heard that had him on alert.

"I heard gunfire." Jumping up, he was already reaching for his pants, not even bothering with his boxers. Pulling on his shirt, he left it unbuttoned and grabbed his gun.

Nervously, I watched him walk to the door and crack it open enough to look out. Light streamed in and amplified the sounds outside. A scream filled the air, and I was on my feet, pulling on my shirt and panties. I struggled to get into my jeans, since they were half inside out.

When I touched Ben's back, he glanced down at me. "I have to check this out. Stay here—"

"No way. I'm coming with you."

Gunshots sounded from what seemed like inside the clubhouse now, and I gulped. "My family is here. I'm not staying locked in this room when they need me."

His brown eyes darkened, but he nodded. "Stay behind me, and do as I say. No matter what." I pressed my lips together, and he tapped me on the ass with his free hand. "No matter what, Lexa, or you stay here."

"Fine. I promise." His brows lifted. "No matter what, I'll stay behind you." I gave in.

"Come on, then," he muttered unhappily.

Another gunshot sounded just down the hall, and I heard a cry. Recognizing the voice as one of the sheep, I clutched at the back of Ben's shirt to keep from running past him to get to her.

"She's not here," India said. "Lexa is home."

"Don't lie to me, bitch. I saw her come here hours ago, and she never left." Ben got to the end of the hall and pressed his back to the wall, his gun aimed and at the ready while he held me back with his other hand. "Now tell me where she is, or I'm going to shoot you again."

"Sh-she and her mom left n-not twenty minutes ago," India continued to lie. "Shh-she went home, I t-tell you."

The pop from the gun going off had me covering my mouth to drown out my scream, tears already running down my face. I loved India. She was so sweet and had always been kind to me. How many times had she babysat me and my brother over the years?

Ben grasped my arm, giving it a squeeze in an attempt at comfort, but there was no time for that. Heavy footsteps were coming our way. But he still held on to my arm with his free hand as he lifted his gun higher and pointed it right at the man who came into view.

"Stop right there," Ben told him, his voice icy cold and deadly. He moved in front of me, blocking me completely with his large body before the man could see us.

But I'd already caught sight of the guy, had committed his image to memory, and I knew I would know him anywhere. Blood and something else were splattered across his face and the stark-white dress shirt he was wearing. An assault rifle in his hands he already had aimed at Ben's chest. His face was classically handsome even for a man of his age. But it was his eyes that had truly terrified me.

They were cold. Dead.

Just like Enzo Fontana's had been.

"Carlo Santino, I presume," Ben greeted, and I clutched at his shirt so tightly, my fingers started to go numb.

"I'm here for the girl," he replied. "I know she's behind you. Just move out of the way, and I won't kill you, copper. Stand in my way, and your beloved grandmother won't recognize you when I'm done."

"Fuck off," Ben snarled. "You're not touching her."

"I don't want to touch her, boy. She's a present to my adopted son. Maybe little Lexa remembers his father—Enzo."

Oh God.

I squeezed my eyes closed. Hearing that name out loud always did something to me. Flipped a switch and took me back to the day I'd nearly died. Ben must have sensed the change in me, because his arm came around, pressing me tighter to him, pulling me back from the memories of that sick sonofabitch beating me until I was unconscious.

"I promised Gian I would gift him the child of the woman who killed his father for his twenty-first birthday. He probably would have taken any of the female children running around this godforsaken place. He's particularly taken with the lovely little twins I've shown him surveillance of."

Oh God.

No. Not Mila and Monroe. He couldn't touch them. Not him, and especially not the monster I just knew Gian must be. If he was even half as evil as his father, he would take the greatest joy in hurting the girls and get off on their pain.

"But I told him Lexa was the one he wanted. And you're standing in my way."

I shifted, needing to know what was going on in front of me, and I peeked at Santino from around Ben's arm. His hand on my back jerked me out of sight once again, but not before I'd seen the rifle pointed right at Ben's chest.

Tears burned my eyes. I couldn't let Santino kill Ben. And I sure as hell couldn't take the chance of him snatching the twins if he couldn't get me.

"If… If I come with you willingly, will you promise not to kill anyone else?" I called out to him.

"Shut up, woman," Ben growled at me. "You're not going anywhere."

"I won't let him hurt anyone else," I whispered. "Especially not you."

"Lexa, I swear on all that is holy, I'm going to tan your beautiful ass as soon as this is over."

"Yes," Santino finally answered, amusement thick in his voice. "You have my word that no one else will be harmed."

"How can I trust you?" I demanded, ignoring Ben's death grip on my hip now. "I don't even know how many you've already killed."

"Think of it this way, *cara*," he reasoned. "How many more people will I kill if you don't come peacefully?"

"She's not going anywhere, motherfucker."

I jerked at the sound of my brother's voice, then one more gunshot was fired off, making me scream.

"Max!"

To my surprise, Ben let me go when I took off running, but I couldn't make sense of what I was seeing. Santino was lying facedown between my brother and me, blood and what looked like brain matter on the floor. There was a gun in Max's hands that hung at his side, his breathing labored as he glared down at the dead body at his feet.

I grabbed him, running my hands over his arms, his chest, making sure he was unharmed, tears streaming down my face. "What were you thinking?" I scolded. "You could have been killed."

"Mom followed Dad back to the house, saying some shit about being pissed at him but loving him too much, and she told me to take care of you. She would have killed me if I'd let that bastard get his hands on you." His free arm wrapped around me, holding on tight. "And your crazy ass was just going to let him take you? What the fuck were *you* thinking, Lexa?"

Ben eased the gun out of Max's hold. "Let me take care of this, yeah?" he said in a calm voice. "Great job taking that piece of shit out, little brother."

"You going to arrest me now, Sheriff?" Max asked with a smirk. That alone told me he was going to be okay, and I sagged against him in relief.

"Not today, kid," Ben said with a wink at me. Tucking the gun into the back of his jeans, he wrapped his arms around both me and my brother, and surprisingly, Max let him. It was then I realized just how hard it was hitting my kid brother. He'd taken a life to save both mine and Ben's, and he didn't know how to feel about it. "I don't know how your parents have survived this long if they have to deal with this shit from you two on a daily basis."

I felt Ben's lips touch the back of my head, and I leaned into him.

The three of us were still like that when Mom and Dad ran into the clubhouse minutes later with all my uncles, their guns drawn and ready for a showdown that was already over.

"Who took out Santino?" Uncle Spider asked as he crouched down beside the dead body.

"That would be me," Max muttered, jaw clenched as he waited for Dad to lose his mind.

Instead, Dad jerked Max against him in a bear hug that should have crushed every bone in his body. "Are you okay?" Dad choked out. "You're not hurt?"

"No, Dad, jeesh. Relax."

"Maybe a little more explanation is in order," Mom said, taking in the carnage she'd missed out on. "There are five dead brothers outside, along with six of Santino's men. India…" She swallowed hard. "India is dead."

Fresh tears burned my eyes, but I told Mom what happened—minus the sex right before we heard the gunfire. Not that Mom didn't suspect. She was eyeing my hair and Ben's unbuttoned shirt, but she didn't comment on it.

"Are you fucking telling me my girls were on this bastard's radar?" Uncle Spider exploded. "And this little shit Gian is interested?"

"That was what Santino said," I confirmed, leaning weakly against Ben.

It was a wonder the building didn't blow up with the force of Uncle Spider's rage. Cursing viciously, he left a trail of fire behind him as he ran outside. Moments later, the powerful engine of his motorcycle roared to life, and he was gone.

"Flick and Rory are in the panic room," Mom said, relieved, looking down at her phone when she got a text. But then she was glaring at me. "Which was where you should have gone as soon as you heard the gunfire. You know the rules."

"I wasn't letting Ben go out there alone," I told her. "And you shouldn't have gone chasing after Dad. You just had surgery. You're going to hurt yourself and put your health at risk before you even start chemo. Are you trying to give us all a heart attack?"

"Yeah," Dad and Max seconded.

"This isn't about me—"

"Everything is about you!" I yelled. "You are the glue that holds this family together, and you have only put yourself at risk all day. Until you get the all clear from the doctor, you're not doing shit from now on!"

Mom's lips twitched for a few seconds before she actually smiled. "And that is how the princess becomes the future queen."

TWENTY-TWO

It was dawn before everything was cleaned up and the bodies were taken away, including Santino's. Everyone gave their statement on what happened, with one minor change to the story.

Max didn't kill Santino.

I did.

After discussing it with them, I told them I didn't want that on Max's record, self-defense or not. It would follow him everywhere. When my deputies showed up, I told them I was the one who shot Santino because he was about to kill Lexa. No one batted an eye; no one questioned me.

Being the sheriff had its perks at times.

Now I was bone-tired and ready for bed, but not without Lexa beside me.

Holding out my hand to her, I held my breath, wondering if the time of her second-guessing me was over. Without hesitation, she wrapped her fingers around mine and waved to her parents. "Night, everyone."

"Night, sweetheart," Raven called after us. "Ben, drive carefully."

"Night, Davis," Bash said with a nod. "Night, baby girl."

Opening the passenger door to my truck, I helped her inside then leaned in to kiss her. "I know you're mine, but do *you* understand that now?"

Her chilled fingers touched my jaw, a tired smile teasing at her lips. "Let's go home, Ben."

"Lexa…"

"I know I'm yours. And I finally realized that you're mine too." She stroked her thumb over the scruff on my chin. "I was scared. I hate admitting it, but yeah, I was. I let everyone get in my head…including your grandmother. But tonight, I finally stopped being scared. The fear of losing you outweighed the fear of you breaking my heart."

"Baby—"

"I trust you, Ben. With my life—and my heart." Cupping the back of my head, she pulled me in for another kiss. "Now, please, take me home."

Grinning, I touched my lips to the tip of her nose. Everything she'd just said was what I'd been aching to hear from her. "Whatever you want, beautiful."

The drive to my apartment took us right past Aggie's, and I stopped really quick to grab us some breakfast sandwiches and coffee. I couldn't even remember the last time I ate, and I could hear her stomach from across the cab of the truck, so I knew she was starving too.

When I came out with the two large coffees and the bag of food, she was leaning her head against the passenger window, sound asleep.

Putting down everything in my hands, I rearranged her so she was more comfortable, and I kissed her forehead before driving us home.

Leaving the food in the truck, I carried her up to my apartment—our apartment—and placed her in bed. Pulling off her shoes and jeans, I tucked the covers up around her and sat on the edge of the bed for a few minutes, just taking in the sight of her where she truly belonged.

After eating, I showered and finally climbed into bed beside her. As my body pressed into hers, she sighed my name in her sleep and turned over, wrapping herself around me like it was the most natural thing in the world to do. As if she'd been doing it all her life.

The events of the day before faded from my memory, and the muscles in my body relaxed one by one.

This was my peace.

Having my woman cuddled up against me, knowing she was safe and I could touch and kiss her whenever the hell I wanted... It was my serenity.

And Lexa was my salvation...

The feel of warm lips against my bare chest had me reaching for her before I'd even opened my eyes. But she evaded my hands with a sexy little giggle and moved farther down my body, her lips leaving a blazing-hot trail in her wake.

I hadn't bothered with clothes after my shower, and when she got to my cock, her hand wrapped around it without hesitation half a second before her mouth swallowed half of my throbbing dick.

Groaning, I tangled my fingers in her long, jet-black hair, silently begging her to take more. The tip hit the back of her throat, and she gagged for a moment, but she didn't pull back. Instead, she sucked in a deep breath through her nose and relaxed her throat, taking all of me.

Her mouth, tongue, and her soft-as-silk hands explored me until I couldn't take it anymore. Grabbing her waist, I flipped her onto her back and tore her panties away. I wanted to thrust into her hard and deep, but remembering that she was probably sore and tender after the night before, I forced myself to take my time, slowly sinking into her tight heat inch by inch until she was squirming under me and begging for it harder.

"I don't want to hurt you," I said between gritted teeth, sweat beading on my brow and rolling down my spine from the restraint of holding myself back from taking her how I really wanted to.

She wrapped her legs around my hips, lifting her ass off the bed as she urged me deeper. "You won't. I can take you. Please, Ben. I need it hard."

Cursing, I gave her exactly what she wanted until she was screaming my name and begging me to never stop. "I love you," I whispered against her ear as her pussy contracted over and over around my cock.

Her lashes lifted, those glacier-blue eyes seeing straight into my soul for the very first time. "I love you too."

Four little words. That was all it took, and I was suddenly exploding deep inside her sweet paradise. "Lexa!" I shouted her name, unable to hold back any longer.

When I could finally remember where I was, I realized I was practically smothering her with most of my weight pressing her into the bed. But she wasn't complaining. Her fingertips were running up and down my sides in a soothing kind of way that, when mixed with the euphoria of having just come inside her, was putting me in a catatonic state.

I lifted my head and started to take my weight off her, but she wrapped her legs tighter around me. "Don't go," she purred. "I love this."

"Let me make you more comfortable." Brushing a soft kiss over her lips, I rolled off her and onto my back, pulling her with me so it was me who was holding her and rubbing her back.

I felt her smile against my chest. "You're right. This is definitely much better."

Smiling contentedly, I kissed the top of her head. "Thought you might like it, beautiful."

"Lucky for you, I'm on the shot," she mumbled sleepily. "You didn't seem to think much about protection yesterday or today, Sheriff."

"Maybe I did think about it and said to hell with it," I suggested vaguely, and her head snapped up, all traces of sleepiness gone.

She glared down at me. "Really?"

I lifted a shoulder in a half shrug. "No, I was too far gone both times to even think about it. But it didn't bother me to think about having sex without a condom like it would have in the past. The thought of being linked to you for life with a baby… I'd be okay with that."

Her eyes widened. "Don't take this the wrong way, okay?" I nodded, already expecting what she was about to say. "Babies are great. One day, I would love to be a mom. But that isn't anytime soon. Please tell me you understand that. I have to finish college, and my mom is sick right now. Although she acts like she can take on the world single-handedly, she's going to need me in the coming months."

"But you're not saying no?"

She nodded. "I'm not saying no. Maybe we can revisit later down the road." She crossed her arms on top of my chest and rested her chin on them, a smile lifting all the way to her beautiful eyes.

I combed my fingers through her hair. "A baby would be a big distraction right now. And we should wait until we're married..." Her head snapped up again, her mouth falling open, making me laugh. "What? Did you think I would just let you be my baby mama and not put a ring on your finger?"

"Baby mama," she repeated with a snort. "That just sounds so weird coming out of your mouth. But no, actually, marriage hadn't even crossed my mind. We haven't even known each other that long. And yet here you are, talking about putting a ring on it and making babies. Slow down for a second and let us enjoy being a couple first, Sheriff."

"I can give you all the time you need on the whole baby subject, Lexa, but on this, I can't." I skimmed my thumb over her bottom lip. It was still swollen from when she was sucking my dick so damn good. "I know it's quick and it's insane, but I also know I'm going to love you for the rest of my life."

"Ben…" She bit her lip, hesitation evident on her face.

And that only made me panic. "Don't say no," I pleaded. "We can compromise on this. You don't have to answer me yet. I'll wait until after your mom is done with chemo, and then I'll propose."

The hesitation disappeared, and she released her lip so she could grin down at me, making it easier for me to breathe again. "You really are insane. But I love you. And I know that I will love you for the rest of my life."

Hearing her repeat the same words I'd said to her only a moment before eased the panic, and I flipped her under me. "Say it again," I commanded as I thrust into her soaked pussy.

She grinned wickedly up at me. "Say what?"

"Lexa," I growled, nipping at her neck.

"I love you," she moaned as my teeth sank into her shoulder. "Oh fuck. I love you."

TWENTY-THREE

The pounding on the front door pulled me from a deep sleep. Groaning, I lifted my head, noticing Ben wasn't in bed beside me.

The pounding came again, and I jumped to my feet, irritated by the intrusion to my sleep. If it was one of my family, I was going to throw them down the stairs.

Except for Mom. I wouldn't throw Mom down them, I reasoned. But Dad or Max, yeah, they were going down the damn stairs.

The room was dark, and I didn't know where any of my clothes were. While the person at the door continued to pound away, I stumbled to the closet and grabbed the first shirt I touched. It was an old T-shirt from the feel of how soft the material was. I pulled it over my head, but I wasn't a dainty little thing, and it just barely covered my ass, even though it was baggy. Stumbling around a little more, I found the dresser and pulled out a pair of Ben's boxer briefs.

I pulled them up as I walked through the living room, and no sooner were they covering my ass than I was jerking the door open. "What?" I snapped, before my eyes adjusted to the setting sun and I realized who was standing in front of me.

Mrs. Davis.

Shit.

I cringed and stepped back, ready to slam the door and run and hide in embarrassment. After what had happened the day before, this woman finding me dressed in her grandson's clothes with wild sex hair and no bra was not how I'd wanted our next meeting to go. Especially now that Ben and I were officially together.

"Hello, Lexa dear," Hannah Davis greeted in that sweet old-lady kind of voice, and all the manners my mom and aunts instilled in me surfaced in a heartbeat.

"Hello, Mrs. Davis. How are you, ma'am?" I was able to mumble loud enough for her to hear, while looking anywhere but at her.

The sound of a vehicle pulling into the parking lot below caught my attention, and I nearly passed out with relief when I realized it was Ben. He opened his truck door and stepped out, carrying two huge bags from Aggie's.

"Gran," he greeted with a scowl as he climbed the stairs. "What are you doing here?"

She pressed her lips together, her shoulders lifting in a small shrug that looked vulnerable to me. "After yesterday, I felt like I owed you an apology in person, honey. You and Lexa both, actually."

As soon as he reached the top of the stairs, I snatched the bags out of his hands, barely noticing the smell of the mouth-watering food as I muttered I would put the meal on the table.

When he met my gaze, his expression softened, and he nodded before taking my place in the open door without allowing his grandmother to come inside. I hurried into the kitchen, pulling the food from the bags without giving it much thought.

Something was smeared on the pie container, and I licked it away at the same time the scent of peanut butter hit me and I finally realized what I was holding. A voice in my head was screaming *danger* even as I began to panic.

Aggie's famous peanut butter pie.

The clear pie package fell onto the floor at my feet with what was a loud *splat* to my ears. "Ben!" I tried to scream, but my throat was starting to close up, that itchy tickle in my throat already making me cough. "B-Ben!"

"Babe, what's wrong?" he asked as he walked into the kitchen.

My panicked eyes met his just as I felt my lips start to swell.

Oh God, I can't breathe. I can't breathe.

"Fuck," he yelled, taking in the state of my face and the pie on the floor. "I forgot to check the food. Babe, I'm so sorry. That Tabby chick filled my order, and I didn't think… I didn't even order pie!"

I couldn't even talk, let alone feel jealous that Tabby had handled my man's food. She hated me, and the feeling was mutual.

Especially now.

277

"Ben!" Mrs. Davis's stern voice seemed to snap him out of his panic, but it did nothing to alleviate my own. "Where's her EpiPen?"

"Babe?"

"Purse," I mouthed, my lungs already desperate for air they weren't going to get. Tears poured from my eyes, and the world started to get blotchy with black spots. "Ben," I wheezed with the last of the oxygen I had.

His strong arms caught me as I started to fall and, almost immediately, I felt something being stabbed into my outer left thigh, but I was already passing out...

I woke up to the sound of a beeping heart monitor and the annoying feel of oxygen tubes in my nose. Ben was in a chair beside the bed, his hand clutching mine as he snored loudly. I almost smiled, but my lips still felt swollen.

"Feeling better?" Mom's hoarse voice asked from the other side of the bed.

I nodded, not ready to see if I could talk again yet.

She was sitting in a chair identical to Ben's. Her hair was tangled, and her clothes looked wrinkled. That, coupled with the dark circles under her eyes, made me wonder how long she'd been there—how long I'd been there.

"Ben called me on the way to the hospital. Apparently, his grandmother drove you both here while he attempted to keep you breathing. Barely, thanks to the first epi injection Mrs. Davis gave you." She sighed tiredly. "I'm going to have to teach that boy to do better when it comes to your allergic reaction."

"We…" My throat hurt like hell, but I had to defend him to her. "We both panicked."

"I know, honey. I know. He loves you so much, and like I was the first time I witnessed your allergy, he was terrified. But he's gotta be better prepared for the next time. And there will be a next time. Although I hope that is far, far into the future." She gave my other arm a squeeze, and I realized there was an IV in the back of my hand. "That all happened yesterday, by the way. They had to give you a second injection as soon as you got to the ER, and then another one around midnight. It was like no sooner had it worn off than they had to give you another. You've scared a good ten years off my life, baby girl."

"I'm…sorry," I whispered.

"Don't be. It happens every time you have a reaction. I'm just thankful you're okay now." She nodded at Ben again. "And once he calmed down and snapped into action, he saved you. So I don't have to kill him."

"Mom. Don't joke," I begged, too tired to imagine she was doing anything but joking.

Smiling, she stood and then leaned over me, kissing my forehead. "Now that you're awake, I can go home and get some sleep. I'll entrust you to the sheriff for the foreseeable future." She stroked her ice-cold fingers down my cheek, tears filling her eyes. "I'm so glad you're okay."

"Love you," I choked out, and she smiled again before leaving.

I lay there just watching him sleep, thankful he and his grandmother knew what to do to help me. He looked haggard, even in sleep, yet still so beautifully masculine, I couldn't take my eyes off him.

It was a long while after she left before Ben started to stir. His lashes began to lift, and I saw confusion in those brandy-brown eyes for a flicker of a second before reality hit him and his hold on my hand tightened. He jerked upright.

"Baby?" he rasped, his eyes running over me like a physical caress as he brought my hand to his mouth and kissed my knuckles. "How are you feeling?"

"Happy to see you," I murmured, trying to smile. But my lips still felt a little swollen, so I wasn't sure if I pulled it off or not. "What about you?"

"Same, beautiful. Same." Holding my hand like a lifeline, he pressed it to his forehead, closing his eyes. "I'll do better from here on out," he vowed. "I'll never let what happened yesterday happen again."

"Wasn't your fault," I tried to reassure him. Cross-contaminations happened all the time at restaurants. People got distracted and things happened. I'd already learned that the hard way, but I knew the risks of eating takeout.

"Yes, it was. I should have checked the food before I even left Aggie's. But all I could think about—" He broke off, his jaw clenching as he glared at the wall in front of him.

"All you could think about?" I urged him to finish.

"I'd just left you sound asleep. All I wanted to do was get home and surprise you with dinner in bed and spend the rest of the night making love to you." With his free hand, he scratched at the scruff on his jaw. I loved that scruff. "I put your life in danger because I couldn't think about anything but my damn cock."

"I really like your cock, though," I tried to tease, but the dark expression on his face told me I wasn't helping. "Ben, honestly, this wasn't your fault. I remember you saying you didn't even order pie."

"Yeah. Your mom called your aunt Quinn and got Tabby fired." He grimaced. "Tabby said it was a mistake, but I don't think your aunt believed her. Maybe she thought there was a chance you would come into contact with it and it would make you sick. I honestly don't know, but I should have checked the damn bag to make sure—"

"Look at me," I ordered when he started condemning himself again. After a tiny hesitation, his gaze met mine, and my heart broke when I saw the sheen of tears in his eyes. "The first time I had a reaction in front of my mom, she'd just gotten back from the grocery store. She'd taken a sample from the little table, and it had been fried in peanut oil. When she picked me up from school, she kissed me on the cheek, not realizing what she'd just eaten. It took fifteen minutes before the reaction set in, but it was bad when it did. She freaked out, and it was my dad who had to inject the epi because she couldn't stop screaming. She blamed herself for weeks. It broke my heart every time I saw the guilt and tears in her eyes."

"Lexa—"

I held up my free hand, stopping him. "I'm going to come into contact with nuts again, Ben. It's inevitable. You just have to be prepared when it does happen. Okay?"

He was quiet for a long moment before finally blowing out a heavy sigh and nodding. "Yeah, baby. Okay."

My teeth sank into my bottom lip for a second before I forced myself to ask the question screaming in my head. "You still want to be with me?"

"You think I wouldn't want to be with you because of this?" he demanded, sounding pissed.

I shrugged weakly. "Some people can't handle being with someone who has serious health issues. If you can't deal with this, tell me now."

"You've said a lot of hurtful things to me in the past, Lexa, but this is beyond belief. I fucking love you. Nothing will ever make me not want to be with you. Without you, I'm an empty shell." Releasing my hand, he cupped my face, his eyes angry but still full of love. "Yesterday scared the hell out of me. I thought I was going to lose you. But I'm not going to walk away from what I feel for you because of it."

"P-Promise?" I whispered, blinking back tears.

When he saw how close I was to breaking, his anger disappeared. "I promise. You're stuck with me, beautiful. Even if your mom killed me, I'd still stick around and haunt you just so I could be with you."

"Don't joke about that," I begged, fighting a grin even as the tears spilled from my eyes.

"She wouldn't off me," he said with a wink. "Raven knows I'd give my life for yours. She seems to like me pretty well. I was sure she would at least threaten me when she got here yesterday, but she was my rock while we waited for you to wake up. Tabby, on the other hand... I'm a little worried for her well-being."

"Good," I muttered half under my breath, but he still heard me and smirked.

"Jealous?"

"Of that cow?" I growled, then sighed. "Yeah. A little. She probably gave you the pie to flirt with you. No doubt she thought if she gave you free pie, you'd want something...more."

"You have nothing to be jealous of. I only want you." His smirk dropped, his eyes turning serious. "I love you and will only ever love you."

My heart melted at his vow, but I still needed to be honest. "I love you too. But I'm going to be jealous of any woman who looks twice at you. Sorry, but when it comes to you, I don't share well."

He winked again and retook my hand so he could kiss my palm. "Same, baby. Same."

EPILOGUE

SIX MONTHS LATER

Holding my breath, I waited for Dr. Weller to give us the results of Mom's latest blood work. Mom sat between Dad and me, holding both our hands. More like the two of us clung to her hands. We were practically shaking with nerves and anticipation, waiting for these results.

Mom gave me a grim smile, her skin finally getting back its healthy glow. Every time I saw how short her hair was, I wanted to cry, but I kept on the brave face I'd learned to perfect while she'd gone through her intense chemo treatments. When she'd started losing her hair, she'd simply shrugged it off, picked up a pair of clippers, and shaved her head.

The next day, all of my aunts had done the same. Flick, Willa, Quinn, Gracie, and Kelli had all been just as bald as Mom, and she'd laughed at the sight of them. When I'd picked up the clippers to do the same, though, Mom had screamed and finally started crying, forbidding me from so much as touching a single strand of my own hair. This shit was taking too much from her, she'd sobbed as I'd held her. It wasn't going to take anything from me too.

Other than that one breakdown, however, she'd been the strong one throughout everything. Even when she was so sick she could barely lift her head from the chemo, she was still the one keeping the rest of us from falling apart because it hurt so damn bad to watch her go through it and be unable to do anything to help her.

The day she rang the bell announcing her last treatment, I'd gone home and cried in Ben's arms for hours, thankful it was over. But still, I was terrified, dreading the results of this test when we would find out if the cancer was gone once and for all.

Dr. Weller was looking over the lab results and not speaking, and I felt bile lift into the back of my throat, shooting Dad a scared look over Mom's head. His blue eyes were just as freaked as my own, and I switched hands with Mom so I could reach behind her and touch Dad's shoulder. His free hand covered mine, holding on just as tightly to it as his other held on to Mom's.

"Okay, well," Dr. Weller finally spoke, and when she looked up, she was grinning from ear to ear. "Everything looks great, Raven. The chemo really was mostly a precautionary measure, and from all these numbers, it looks like you are cancer-free. Congratulations."

Dad let out a choked sound and jumped to his feet, his shoulders already shaking as the door slammed behind him. I bit my lip, trying not to cry, but I was so damn happy, I couldn't contain the tears.

Mom only smiled at the doctor. "Thanks for everything, Doctor," she said as she shook the woman's hand and stood.

"I hope you'll be an advocate now to make sure every woman you know gets yearly screenings," the doctor said with a stern lift of her brows.

"Trust me, she is," I said with a shaky laugh. She'd even been on my case lately to get my yearly exam, but I already had to keep my yearly appointments to make sure I got my birth control shots anyway. Still, it had freaked me out this last time, because I'd been scared it would come back that something was wrong.

Outside, we found Dad sitting in the SUV. His eyes were swollen and bloodshot, but he'd gotten himself under control. Mom and I don't say anything to him about it, because really, I was still having trouble containing myself too. I'd never felt relief so strong in my life. All I wanted to do was laugh and cry at the same time.

Mom was okay.

She wasn't sick anymore.

We weren't going to lose her.

"I'm hungry," Mom commented while Dad pulled into traffic. "Let's grab some lunch."

"Whatever you want, baby," Dad said in a hoarse voice.

From the back seat, I watched her reach for his hand. He linked his fingers through hers and placed their hands on his thigh. Seeing them like this, it made my heart happy. Even after all these years, they were still so in love, so attuned to each other's feelings that they didn't need words to express themselves.

I wanted that same thing twenty, fifty, a hundred years down the road with Ben.

Aggie's was so crowded when we got there, it was almost impossible to find a place to park. On the drive, I'd finally gotten myself under control and had texted both Max and Ben to let them know Mom was cancer-free. I was all smiles as I walked with my parents into the diner, still looking at my phone, reading the last text Ben had sent after I'd told him the good news.

Ben: Let's celebrate tonight.

I was typing out a reply as we walked through the door, so when everyone shouted, I jerked in surprise and nearly dropped my phone.

I hadn't even noticed whose cars and motorcycles were in the parking lot, so hearing all my family members congratulating Mom had startled me. Mom was pulled into a group hug with her brothers, then her sisters-in-law and Aunt Willa, before Uncle Spider was twirling Mom around and around, making her laugh.

Smiling at the happiness on everyone's faces, I stepped around them and sat at the counter, waiting.

"Hi."

At the sound of Ben's voice, I glanced up, surprised and delighted to find him standing beside me. "Hi," I purred and started to stand so I could kiss him.

But with a hand on my shoulder, he pushed me back onto the stool and turned me to face away from everyone else while he leaned on the counter beside me.

"Right here," he said as he shook his head, a grin teasing at his lips. "It was right here that I saw you for the first time. I sat there." He pointed at the booth he'd been in the night we'd met. "Do you remember?"

"I'll never forget," I whispered, a feeling of nostalgia hitting me. "That night changed everything."

His brandy-brown eyes locked with mine. "And then I kissed you a little later, and I knew."

Smiling, I lifted a brow at him. "Knew what, Sheriff?"

"That I wanted to spend the rest of my life with you."

"That soon?"

His thumb traced over my bottom lip. "That soon," he confirmed. "I love you."

Catching his hand, I linked our fingers together. "I love you too."

"Lexa—"

But I covered his mouth with my hand before he could even start.

"Yes," I breathed, fresh tears filling my eyes because I knew what he was about to ask. Had known it was coming. I didn't mean to steal his thunder, but I didn't need him to speak the words to know he was going to propose. "Yes, Ben."

He swallowed hard and pulled me up, kissing the breath out of me, while behind us, the rest of my family was still celebrating Mom's amazing news.

"You mean it?" he demanded when he finally lifted his mouth barely half an inch.

"I'd marry you tomorrow if that's what you want," I promised, my laugh a little shaky from my continued happy tears. "I love you. I want to be your wife."

He kissed me again, quicker this time, before glancing in my mom's direction. "Maybe give her a little time to take this all in before we start planning the wedding. So, like, two weeks?"

Laughing happily, I hugged his waist. "Deal."

COMING NEXT

Rockers' Legacy Series

Holding Mia August 27th

Sons of the Underground

Off Limits Coming Soon

CPSIA information can be obtained
at www.ICGtesting.com
Printed in the USA
BVHW030248190421
605284BV00015B/371